"Now let's set the record straight. It was three or four girls each time, in pants and pullovers, at most of the kidnappings and at these flash public killings. Was it the same women each time?"

"We don't think so."

"Is Lady Day a person or a movement?"

"Probably both. The methods, the uniform clothes. This sounds like one of those militant women's outfits out of the 1960s and 70s — only more out of hand."

After Things Fell Apart

RON GOULART

BERKLEY BOOKS, NEW YORK

All characters in this book are fictitious.
Any resemblance to actual persons, living or dead,
is purely coincidental.

AFTER THINGS FELL APART

A Berkley Book / published by arrangement with
the author

PRINTING HISTORY
Ace edition / October 1977
Berkley edition / April 1985

ISBN: 0-425-07647-4

A BERKLEY BOOK® TM 757,375
Berkley Books are published by The Berkley Publishing Group,
200 Madison Avenue, New York, New York 10016.
The name "BERKLEY" and the stylized "B" with design are
trademarks belonging to Berkley Publishing Corporation.
PRINTED IN THE UNITED STATES OF AMERICA

I

THE MONEY HAD just been piled on the desk when the earthquake came. Jim Haley slapped a hand over it and waited for the swaying to stop. The office coffee machine hopped off its stand, bounced twice along the bank of data boxes and hit the floor. Unground soy beans tumbled out of its side and began jiggling on the vinyl. The walls of the building groaned faintly and odd sounds came from the lagoon.

"These quakes always scare the swans," said Darnell McGuinness. He ran and braced himself in the open door. Glossy photos, microcards and the canvas petty cash bag clutched against his sweatered chest. A big round-edged man.

The thousand dollars crackled less under Haley's hand. "Not a bad one this time." He was tall and lean, all bones and weather-tanned skin. Under thirty with unobtrusive brown hair cut, hastily, short.

McGuinness was watching the wide, tree surrounded lagoon outside. "Nothing ruffles those seagulls." He stepped out onto the gravel, then bent to the right and squinted. "It's still . . ." he began.

"Arf, arf," said one of the data boxes.

5

"Your data box is barking," Haley called at the doorway.

"Too many earthquakes. It makes them goofy. Ignore it. Where was I? Yes, I was remarking that it's still there and intact."

Haley fished his flat wallet out of his inside jacket pocket and filled it with money. The quake seemed about over. "What is?"

"The Golden Gate Bridge," said the Chief of the Intelligence and Investigation Office. "I remember the big San Francisco quake of 1976. A lot of people thought the bridge would fall that time. Well, I've never really liked bridges. Or the Bay itself, for that matter. But the government of San Francisco Enclave insists on our keeping our offices in the Palace of Fine Arts here. A small fortune was spent restoring this dreadful building and nobody wants to abandon it." He crossed back to his desk as the quake gave a final dim rumble. "We're much too close to the water, historic landmark or not."

"Woof woof," said the third data box from the left.

Haley returned his wallet to his inside pocket. He left his chair and bent over the fallen coffee machine. "Didn't somebody propose filling in the lagoon at the last meet of the S.F. Enclave governing board?"

"Oh, I like this lagoon. It's artificial," said Chief McGuinness. "San Francisco Bay and the Pacific Ocean are what annoy me. I keep expecting a tidal wave."

"You actually lived down in the Republic of Southern California for awhile, didn't you?" said Haley.

He righted the machine and scooped up the scattered soy beans.

"Bow wow," said the same data box.

"The earthquakes jiggle them out of whack," said Chief McGuinness. "It's no use requesting a repair man. That takes a month. So I usually fix them myself. There's a little manual that came with them. These are the old Datzrite/3000 models. In the manual it explains, you know, what all the different malfunctions are. I forget what barking means. Last week one of them was whistling like a canary bird and that means a blown fuse."

"Can't you look in the repair manual?"

"I filed it in one of the data boxes and now they won't give it back to me," explained McGuinness. "What were you asking me? Oh, about the Republic of Southern California. Yes, I more or less lived there. Nobody can really live down there. It was like that even before the Chinese Commandos invaded and everything fell apart. You're too young to remember that."

Haley, as he sat down again, pointed at the photos McGuinness was still clutching. "Why did you send for somebody from the Private Inquiry Office?"

"Back to business, right." The chief dropped into his chair, spread out six pictures of dead men. "I'm glad PI sent you, Jim. You're efficient, know how to get information. Though you're a little too eccentric. There's another PI man nearly as good as you, but he's too horny. La Penna."

Haley grinned, which gave his face a momentarily sunken look. "You want me to work on the Lady Day thing, don't you?"

McGuinness had been studying the photos upside down. He swallowed and nodded his head. "You've heard the name?"

"Sure, but nothing concrete," said Haley. "I move around outside of S.F. a lot, through most of the Enclave controlled counties. Down as far as Big Sur and over to the Napa Valley and the San Joaquin. I've heard the name, heard it linked with these killings." Haley absently touched the place in his coat where the money was. "Enclave police can't handle this?"

Chief McGuinness said, "The cops are not usually too successful outside of San Francisco proper. There have been other killings beside these in the city. This Lady Day business has spread out all over Northern California. An organization like the Private Inquiry Office, financed in part by private money—agricultural money, I hear—you can do things the police can't. Get information, buy it, in places cops aren't welcome. We've got to stop this slaughter of our prominent men."

Haley brought the photos into one pile. "Professor Takahashi," he said of the top photo. "Kidnapped from his office in the ruins of old S.F. State and then shot the following day on the revolving bar at the Fairmont Hotel. Three girls, masked, wearing black clothes, did it, according to witnesses." He turned to the next picture. "Admiral Burly, retired. He was set fire to in Children's Storyland at Frisco Zoo."

"You younger people say Frisco, I notice," put in

Chief McGuinness. "That was a taboo when I was a kid. A carryover from when we'd been part of the state of California, part of the U.S.A."

Haley shuffled through the rest of the photos, stopped at the sixth. "Hey, this is Fortalanza, from the S.F. governing board itself. When was he killed?"

McGuinness blinked. "Only this morning. Stabbed in the parking lot of Grace Cathedral during an outdoor seance." Reluctantly the chief reached out and pushed one of the yellow buttons inset along the lefthand side of his desk. "The information on his death is in one of the data boxes. Excuse me, Jim, I'll have to use them." He poked at the button again.

A data box, half man size and gunmetal in color, rolled out of line and across the purple vinyl floor. "Arf, arf," it said.

"I knew I'd get that one."

The square box rolled over Haley's left foot and bumped into the Chief's desk. "Data Box 45A reporting for duty, bow wow."

"Stop that silly barking." McGuinness scowled at the data box's slightly askew speaker grid. "Give us what you have on the assassination of Dante B. Fortalanza."

"That's a good subject," said the box. "Now, I've been worrying a lot about these killings and about the senseless violence rampant in our culture in general. The problem is, everyone these days is too cerebral. I think we need a turning back to the simple virtues of the past, a turning back to the glorious days when each citizen of San Francisco was respon-

9

sible for law enforcement. In those golden vigilante days of yore it was relatively—"

Chief McGuinness kicked the box in the side. "Give us the damn data and don't editorialize. Not verbally either. Print me the info."

"Arf arf," replied the data box. "Okay, but you guys ought to listen to what we men in the street have to say." It whirred and dropped a manila folder into the wire basket attached to its right side.

Chief McGuinness snatched up the folder and opened it on his desk top. Three dance bids and a tinted wedding photo were on the top of the data. He examined one of the bids. "S.F. Enclave Free University's Come As Your Favorite Third World Leader Dance, April 5, 1984. What is this stuff?"

Haley stretched and extracted the photo. "This is my mother and father's wedding picture. I didn't know you had a file on me."

"Who are all these other people in the wedding picture?"

"The Free Speech Movement," said Haley. "My folks met at a sit-in at Cal. My father was much more liberal in those days."

"You sure went to a lot of dances, for a criminology major," said the chief. To the data box he said, "Where did you get this material?"

The box said, "Haley, James Sheridan. Born 3 March 1964, Berkeley, California, then U.S.A."

"I don't want to know that."

The box ratcheted. "Directive 5234B requires background material on all operatives working on Intelligence and Investigation Office assignments."

McGuinness gave the box another kick. "Okay, okay, file the damn stuff, then. Now give me what you have on the latest assassination."

The machine whirred and a yellow plastic pistol dropped into its basket.

"I thought you said he was stabbed," said Haley.

"Yes. That's apparently one of your old toys, Jim," said the chief apologetically. "The guys who do backgrounding for us are awfully thorough."

Haley took up the toy gun, hefted it. His initials were scratched into the handle. "It shot darts with plastic tips."

"We have those, too," the data box told him. "And your baby shoes."

Chief McGuinness snorted and hit another desk button with his balled up fist. The data box rolled back into its place against the wall and made a turning off sound. "I'll simply tell you what we know, Jim, and send you a written report later. I depend too much on these gadgets. I ought to toss them all out. Let's see. Yes, when Fortalanza died he muttered, 'Lady Day.' He also added, 'They're going to take over.'"

"According to the *Examiner-Chronicle*, Judge Vetterlein mumbled a name. I assume it was Lady Day."

"Yes."

"Do you have anything else you've held back? Anything on these Lady Day raiders that wasn't in the paper or on the TV station?"

"Precious little."

"Three or four girls each time, in pants and pullovers, at most of the kidnappings and at these flash public killings." Haley, with one bony hand, placed the photos back on the desk so they faced toward Chief McGuinness. "Was it the same girls each time?"

"We don't think so. Witnesses usually don't agree much, but there's such a variance here I figure we may have as many as a dozen different women involved."

"Women or girls? The paper said they were young."

"Mostly in their early twenties," said the chief. "Girls, yes. From what you've heard, Jim, is Lady Day a person or a movement?"

"Probably both," answered the PI operative. "The methods, the uniform clothes. This sounds like one of those militant women's rights outfits out of the 1960s and 70s, only more out of hand."

"How'd you hear about the 1960s and the 1970s?"

"At SFEFU," Haley said. "I minored in Nostalgia and Pop Culture, which interested me then."

"You've never mentioned it before. We'll have to talk about situation comedies and light shows sometime. Two of my favorite nostalgia topics," said Chief McGuinness. "Some of those female equality people took to killing men in the 70s, though."

"On a small scale. A lot of times for personal reasons. There doesn't seem to be anything like that involved here."

"Right. The only thing linking these dead men is their prominence in S.F. Enclave life." The chief rubbed his elbow. "I'm worried, Jim. There could be a war against men brewing. Six men killed right in San Francisco in the past month, not to mention others in Northern California. Three men killed last week and this and today is only Tuesday."

Haley said, "Okay. What do you want done?"

Chief McGuinness tore the top sheet from a memo pad. "A lead has turned up, Jim. It seems legitimate, though not something our cops can run down too well. Start with this and see where it leads you. Spend as much of that cash as you have to, going places and buying information." He waved the memo slowly a few times. "A man across the Golden Gate Bridge in Olden Town says his niece has been living with his family for the last few weeks. He's certain she was involved with this Lady Day thing and then quit. I'd like you to meet this girl and talk to her." He gave Haley the name and address of the suspicious uncle. "Take all the time you need following this business. Keep in mind the fact that more prominent men will be getting killed while you're investigating. I'm hoping the next time a batch of these girls surfaces the cops can trail them. So far we haven't had any luck there at all. They show, kill, disappear."

Haley grinned his moderately frightening grin and got up. "You're probably not prominent enough to be a target. So relax."

McGuinness said, "The thought does keep occurring to me, Jim. I don't know. Assassins, earthquakes, the ocean. My life seems pretty joyless at times."

"You ought to transfer to an outside job." Haley folded the memo page into his trouser pocket and strode from the office. He'd left his electric motor bike parked and locked up a grassy slope and across the lagoon from the Palace of Fine Arts. He ambled slowly up to the bike, glancing back at the quiet water and at the antique brown domed building, left-over from a long forgotten exposition. It was rich with imitation pillars and draped statuary.

There was a riot in progress on the Golden Gate Bridge when he drove up to it.

II

A PAPER-WRAPPED ROLL of quarters spiraled from the hip pocket of the Enclave policeman as he came diving for Haley's electric motor bike. He slammed down, hard on his knees, next to the ducked over Haley and said, "Sometimes I think our society is too fragmented, Jim."

Rifle balls were whizzing in the misty air. Home-made bombs exploded all around. "Another dispute about the second half of the bridge, huh?" Haley remarked.

The bridge cop said, "This week the Fort Baker bunch are supposed to run the half of the bridge that doesn't belong to the S.F. Enclave. But those guys from Black Sausalito claim they missed a turn last Easter and they want to collect secondary tolls this week."

The row of cars trying to leave San Francisco was twenty vehicles long and a man in about the tenth car, a vintage gas engine Mustang, jumped out angrily. He tugged at a six shooter in the side pocket of his business jumpsuit, shouting, "Why can't all this factionalism be ended?" He wrenched the revolver completely free and waved it in the direction of Haley and the cop.

They both shrugged, the cop calling, "Put away that weapon or I'll have to arrest you."

"I'm a doctor," said the blond man. "I have to carry a gun when I make house calls over to Marin County." He gestured at the fogged over country across the orange bridge. "The head of the San Anselmo Amateur Mafia is having a serious attack of asthma right now."

"Tell them," said the cop. He nodded at the hundred or so men struggling on the span. "Too much splitting up," he said to Haley. "Those Natty Bumpo Brigade guys from Fort Baker and the Black Sausalito crew and the Amateur Mafia and the real Mafia. Too much splitting up."

"You have to learn to relax," Haley told him. He left the safety of the far side of his stopped motor bike and ran, bent low, to the angry doctor. "You have your medical bag and IDs?"

"Of course. Who are you?"

"Haley, PI Office. Pull your car over into the weeds there. Join me on my bike."

When the doctor had done what Haley'd suggested he asked, "Now what?"

Haley indicated the rear rack seat of his bike.

15

"Climb on. Here, give me your doctor's flag." He pulled the white red crossed flag from the medical bag and hooked it over his handlebars. Clicking the electric motor on, Haley drove himself and the doctor toward the first toll gate.

A plump dark boy in a leather fringe suit fell dead in their path just beyond the abandoned glass and metal toll booth. "Pioneer nonsense," said the doctor. "Serves him right."

A black man, taller and even more sharp edged than Haley, retrieved his throwing knife from the dead Natty Bumpo Brigade boy and leaped for Haley's slow moving bike. "Off till we settle this jurisdictional dispute, daddy."

"Relax," Haley told him as he halted the bike. "It's me, Haley. I'm taking this doctor through to San Anselmo."

The black man wiped the knife blade on the leg of his lemon yellow fatigue suit. "Oh, hi, Jim. You're the friend of Norman's. You were on our Soul Food Panel last month."

"One of the judges," said Haley. "And I won an honorable mention in the Mississippi blues harp contest."

"White division. Sure, I recollect you now, daddy. Where's the doctor going to?"

"San Anselmo," the doctor told him. "The head of the Amateur Mafia there may be dying."

"Is he handing me a line of jive, Jim?"

The doctor scowled. "Your anachronistic speech patterns are no more appealing than the frontier affectations of those Fort Baker pricks. You people

16

signed an agreement with the S.F. Enclave Medical Association. Now honor it."

"He sure is dichty." The black man took a red bandanna from around his neck. "Tie this on over your flag, Jim. Safe conduct."

Five young men in buckskin, wearing fur hats, came charging at the black man. Haley scattered them with his onmoving bike. The mist rolled in thicker from the early afternoon Pacific and Haley barely avoided running down two news analysts. The men were stooped behind their overturned and smoldering TV wagon, commenting on the skirmishing.

"I think, Dick, we ought to tell the listeners what just happened," the grayer of the pair said into his hand mike.

"Good idea, Larry," said Dick. He was smoking a pipe. "Some maniacs on a motor bike almost ran us down in the fog."

"The fog is very thick here today, folks," said Larry. "As you saw for yourselves until our cameras were blown up."

"I think, Larry," said Dick, "the fog is even thicker than it was a few minutes ago."

"You may be right," chuckled Larry. "One more reason for both of us to keep on the lookout."

The lank blond doctor had leaped from the halted motor bike and he said now, "Will you media pricks get out of the way? I'm on an emergency call."

"I don't know if you folks can hear this exchange or not," said Dick into his button size palm mike. "One of these maniacs who almost ran us down a minute or so back has now called us media pricks. Oh, and now he's started to pummel Larry with his suitcase. I wish our cameras hadn't been destroyed and you could get a look at this."

"It isn't a suitcase," shouted the angry doctor. He'd knocked the gray newsman over with his medical bag. "I happen to be the public relations director for the SFEMA and this doesn't sit well with me. Now drag your equipment out of the way."

"You can't guess, folks, who just showed up," Dick told his listeners. "One of Frisco Enclave's better known medicos-about-town. I wonder if you'd comment on today's rioting, doctor?"

"S.F. Enclave ought to take a leaf out of the Republic of Southern California's book and take over control of all these experimental colonies in our territory."

"That would hardly be democratic, doctor." Dick had a silver monitoring device inserted in his left ear and it began to buzz faintly. "Sorry, doctor, I'd like to go on with this very interesting discussion but I have to switch back to the station for some up to the minute comment on the Fortalanza assassination. This is Dick Reisberson, KENC News, the middle of the Golden Gate Bridge."

Four young men in buckskin came jumping over the wagon; one was yelping and waving a red bandanna in the air. The other three fired muskets into the mist. Then they stopped, shuffled about, one stumbling against Haley's bike. "Was that okay?" asked the boy who'd yelped.

"Where were you ten minutes ago?" asked the newsman.

"We were hurrying here when some of those jigaboos set fire to our covered wagon."

Dick Reisberson shrugged. He helped his still slightly dazed partner up off the bridge paving. "We're through for today."

"Couldn't we transcribe something for later showing?"

"Not after that idiot leader of yours allowed some of you to blow up our TV wagon," said Dick. "You could take a few lessons from these spades. I had them scheduled for 12:45 and smack at 12:45 five of them came jumping into camera range."

"We live like pioneers," said the spokesman of the Natty Bumpo Brigade men. "We tell time by the sun and moon. And that's tough in fog like today." He rubbed his fur hat nervously over his groin for a moment. "Can't I even read the statement about why we claim this half of the bridge should be ours permanently? How we feel America went off the track politically sometime in August of 1776."

"No, you're too late."

"I guess you don't want the wild turkey we cooked for you, either?"

The doctor growled and jumped into the driver's seat of Haley's bike. "We can squeeze by on the left of this mess. Let's get moving."

Haley ran and landed on the rear seat as the bike skidded around the burned out television equipment. The fighters on the bridge showed only intermittently. Black hands grabbing at coonskin caps, rifles popping and smoking. Knives, traditional and modern, flashing.

Suddenly a heavy black man in a purple pinstripe jumpsuit leaped out of the mist and carried Haley off the rear seat. "You Bumpo jokers going mechanical now?"

Haley was carried clear off the bike and onto the sweaty asphalt. He caught a glimpse of the angry doctor pressing on. "Norman, it's me," he explained from beneath the two hundred and fifty pound Black Sausalito leader.

"Shut my mouth," said Norman. "Excuse me for going upside your head, Jim."

"I'm escorting a doctor to San Anselmo," said Haley while Norman was riding off.

"Appears you was traveling most too slow for him. He's long gone now." Norman studied the thick fog the doctor had ridden away into. "I'll loan you a bicycle, partner. We got a bunch parked just off the bridge. Come on, I'll walk you."

"Can you leave the confrontation?"

"For a few minutes. I already read my demands over the bullhorn, talked to the media, burned up part of the secondary toll booth and knifed five Bumpo jackstroppers. I can take a little break." Norman put an arm around Haley's lean shoulders. "Was that all you were up to, Jim? Taking a medicine man on his rounds don't sound like PI business."

"I'm looking for leads on the Lady Day movement," said Haley. "Have you heard anything lately?"

Norman shook his head quickly. "Nothing shaking there, Jim."

"Don't shit me now."

"I'm not, Jim. Just because Lady Day uses the name of some old spade jazz singer don't mean she's automatically a spade herself, you know."

Haley said, "Okay, relax."

Norman paused for a moment in the mist, then led Haley off to the right. "How's this one here? A ten speed Italian racing bike."

"Too fancy, Norm. I may not return it for awhile." Haley reached out and grabbed an orange and white three speed American style bicycle.

"An antique, but it runs good," Norman observed. "Same color as our bridge, too. Keep it long as you like."

"Maybe a few days." Haley gripped the handlebars. "Hey, by the way, I thought you told me Black Sausalito was going in for more public relations and less fighting."

"Yeah," said Norman, "but these Natty Bumpo jackstroppers keep shooting our Public Relations Directors. One of these days, and it won't be long, we're going to take over that Fort Baker of theirs. And you know how?"

"With a commando raid."

"Man, you got second sight. How you know that?"

"The last time I was over in Black Sausalito I noticed the Free Academy was teaching a course on the Chinese Commandos."

"Right. Those jokers had some good ideas," said the black leader. "The way they snuck up on Southern California like that. That takes chutzpah. Of course, the United States was collapsing. I reckon as how that made it easier. You remember the United States at all?"

"Not much," said Haley. "But we studied it in school."

Norman said, "These Natty Bumpo Brigade jokers, with their skin suits and all the fringe. That's where they belong, down in the Republic of Southern California."

"Remember, the Chinese Commandos didn't win." Haley got a running start and swung into the bicycle seat.

"That's because they had chutzpah," called Norman, "but not soul."

Beyond Black Sausalito and the Fort Baker pioneer colony, as the old 101 Highway climbed inland, the fog stopped. Haley pumped out of it and into bright sunlight. The fields rose away green and rolling and quiet all around him. There was little traffic, a few electric land cars and a scattering of diesel produce trucks. He saw no sign of the doctor who'd swiped his motor bike. Haley grinned a particularly malicious looking grin and pedaled more casually. For a few moments he rode with his arms stretched out at his sides and his face turned up to the sun. He whistled a little.

After almost an hour he turned off the rundown six lane highway and rode around a long out-of-repair cloverleaf until he was on Sir Francis Drake Boulevard. Haley remained on that, passing through a mixture of small towns and colonies, wild flowers and small forests.

Eventually he heard lute music and left the highway to ride over a winding downhill path.

III

A COUNTER-TENOR VOICE came weaving up through the trees. The singer, accompanied by a lute, sang, "O mistress mine, where are you roaming? O mistress mine, where are you roaming?"

Haley rested his bicycle against a tree bole and continued on foot. A big man with a crossbow stepped from behind an oak and into his path. "Hello," said Haley, grinning.

"We don't allow tourists on weekdays," the man said. He wore a forest green tunic and leotard, leather sandals, a scarlet skullcap and a full brownish beard. The tip of his crossbow bolt pointed at Haley's chest.

"O stay and hear your true love's calling," sang the unseen lutist.

"I'm in Olden Town to see a man named Poulton Cruze," Haley explained.

The bow rose and fell slightly in the bearded man's two-handed grip. "From Frisco Enclave, aren't you? I can tell by your garb you're somebody who could exist in that sort of harsh urban setting. Makes no difference. Olden Town is a closed community save on market days, when we allow outlanders in."

Slowly Haley slid his hand into his jacket. "I'm with the Private Inquiry Office and we have an access and extradition agreement with the sheriff of Olden Town." He drew out a five dollar SFE bill, which was blue and yellow and bore the picture of Walter Lippman. "So you can let me pass."

The crossbow dipped and the man said, "We're simple folk here, living in a rustic way. Still, times aren't so good I can turn aside a five dollar bribe." He reached for the money. "The devil is a busy man."

"Yes," agreed Haley; "he should relax more." He walked on down through the high oaks and pines. The singer had stopped. The lute played on, accompanied by a viola and a flute. The woods ended and the homes and shops of Olden Town appeared. The streets were cobbled with buff colored stones, the houses and stores were of plaster and cross hatched wooden beams. Some roofs were of pale tile, others of muddy colored thatch. Fat dogs chased plump cats through narrow lanes. Children in simple tunics played at marbles and mumbletypeg near doorsteps. The men of Olden Town, some two dozen of whom were in evidence in the street, wore tunics, leotards, leggings, cloaks and skullcaps. The few women visible wore long loose garments, their hair braided.

The sheriff of Olden Town was stretched out on a wood bench in front of his Tudor style office, asleep with his bandaged fingers loosely interlocked on his lap. When Haley nudged him the sheriff sat quickly up awake, dropping a carving knife and a small incomplete wooden skull to the cobblestones. "What ho?" he asked, making a chewing sound.

"You dropped your skull," said Haley, handing the carving and the sharp bladed knife back.

"Careful with that knife," cautioned the sheriff. "Oh, hello, Haley. How are you? I'm not getting anywhere with this carving of memento mori knick-knacks."

"I thought you weaved on the side."

The sheriff was a big man in burlap colored tunic and leggings, about thirty-five with prominent red cheeks. "No, I took another aptitude test and they decided I wasn't meant to weave. Just in time, too. I turned out thirty yards of lopsided tartan as it was. Ever tried to hand weave a tartan?"

"No." Haley asked, "Poulton Cruze's shop is on this street, isn't it?"

"Two blocks down," replied the sheriff. "Don't pay attention to the address numbers on the next block. Councilman Ferman painted them before they found out he didn't have any aptitude for numerals. Letters, especially capitals, he's okay. Not numbers."

"Your aptitude people seem to vacillate a lot."

"Not people anymore." The sheriff noticed the carved skull in his hand and set it away at the far end of his bench. "That's spooky. I have enough problems trying to stop some of those Amateur Mafia kids from poaching our forests. But you can't argue with a computer. I think all these earthquakes addled this one. It was secondhand to begin with."

Haley grinned a bony grin. "The town aptitude tester is a computer now?"

Setting his carving knife gingerly aside, the sheriff said, "You look something like a memento mori when

25

you smile. Excuse me, Haley. Everything strikes me spooky today. Yes, the Olden Town council voted to use a computer to pick voluntary chores for us citizens."

"Anachronistic," said Haley, still grinning.

"I know," agreed the sheriff. "Even with the thatch roof they decided to put on it." He yawned, settled back, eyed the bright afternoon sun. "Bribe fee has gone up also."

"How much?"

"I'll have to ask you for thirty dollars from now on." The sheriff noticed his carving knife. "You know how to hold one of these the right way?"

"Yes." Haley gave the sheriff the money, in Adlai Stevenson tens, and demonstrated the right way to grip the knife. Then he strolled to the shop of Poulton Cruze. Cruze was a narrow man of forty, long necked and fuzzy headed. He was dressed all in scarlet. His shop occupied the ground floor of a thin two story building of brown shingle and yellow tile. Its stained glass window carried the words CRUZE: WEAPONRY in gilt.

Cruze was on a redwood stool behind a short counter and behind his shaggy head was an illuminated scroll saying: *Keep up your bright swords, for the dew will rust them*. Cruze squinted his left eye and said, "You're not a tourist."

"I'm Haley, with the Private Inquiry Office. Frisco I&I sent me to talk with you."

Cruze blinked, got off the stool left sidedly. "Oh, yes, yes." He edged around the counter, patted an ornate rapier on display there, and went to the shop's doorway. He closed the door, bolted it, drew down the shade. Inscribed on the shade was: *I will not cease from mental fight, nor shall my sword sleep in my hand, till we have built Jerusalem, in England's green and pleasant land. William Blake (1757-1827).*

Haley removed a bundle of unfletched arrows from an oak chair and sat down, watching Cruze still at the door. "Tell me about your niece."

"Penny's not here anymore," said Cruze. "I have the fear she's gone to live in San Rafael, that dreadful place. A stronghold of Amateur Mafia people, full of twenty-four hour coffee shops and bowling alleys and taco parlors. A town with no silence, no feeling for times past."

"When did she leave?"

"Two days ago," said Cruze. He had an intermittent stammer. "You know, I wrote that letter to your Intelligence and Investigation Office nearly a week ago."

Haley nodded, grinned. Cruze looked away and Haley asked, "Do you know for certain she's in San Rafael?"

"No. I only know the name of the town came up frequently in her arguments with us. It seemed to fascinate her." The stammer lurked in his voice and he seemed for a moment to be about to lose control of his speech entirely. "I really only know she failed to return from work the day before yesterday."

"What's her name and where was she working?"

"Penny. She'd been working as some sort of secretary for the Nixon Institute. It's that historical archives sort of place in San Anselmo. Only a few miles from us here."

"What do they say?"

"Only that she resigned. I hiked up to the vidphone on 101 to call them," said Cruze. "Learned next to nothing."

"Can you give me her full name and a description?"

"Oh, yes. Penny Deacon. Her mother was my sister. Both her parents are dead—the food riots in Santa Ana four years back. Penny's been on her own, on the road most of the time since then. Sometimes she shows up here, stays for a time. Somewhere or other she's managed to pick up a fair enough education." Cruze took a stray arrow in his hand and worked the nock against his cheekbone. "She's a quite pretty girl, even after all she's been through. Tall, slender, with dark hair. I have no pictures, since we don't encourage photographic equipment in Olden Town."

"How old?"

Cruze rubbed with the arrow. "Lord, I guess she's not quite twenty-one even now."

Haley steepled his fingers. "What about Lady Day?"

Resting the arrow on the counter, Cruze said, "My wife, Estrellita, is the one who should tell you this. But there's no use, she won't. She told me and then refused to discuss it further. She's not home now anyway. At the pottery kiln, glazing."

"Penny confided in your wife."

"Yes, isn't that interesting? Women in all ages

and all situations can confide in each other. Letting their hair down is how Estrellita puts it. You see . . . What is your name, did you say?"

"Haley."

"You see, Haley, women have a sentimental side. No matter what sort of knocks they've taken." The stammer had grown worse and Cruze paused to let it pass. "Lord, I suppose Penny's even slept with strange men. So many strangers now. Outside the colonies and the enclaves it's not gentle, Haley."

"What did she tell your wife?" asked Haley.

"No great weapon was ever invented by a woman," Cruze said. "Not to my knowledge. Still, it's interesting, isn't it, to see this Lady Day organization of women quite fond of killing? They sound to be quite weapons oriented."

"Did Penny belong to the Lady Day group?"

Cruze ran his fingers along the rapier blade. "Mankill, Inc."

"That's what the group is called?"

"Pretty explicit, isn't it? It's interesting to me that they've picked a rather melodramatic name. Still, it's explicit, as I said. So far as my wife, Estrellita, could determine they do call themselves that, yes. Penny joined this Mankill, Inc. thing somewhere south of here. About three or four months ago."

"South where?"

"That Penny didn't say."

"And she quit?"

"Apparently after only a few weeks," said Cruze. "She hadn't realized the name was to be taken literally. They didn't right off tell her of their plans to kill all the men."

"All the men."

"Not all exactly. Only the, as Penny says they put it, the opposition. The men in control and those who won't recognize the authority of Lady Day. She wants to kill, then take over."

"Who is Lady Day?"

"Penny won't talk about her."

"But there is a specific person calling herself Lady Day."

Cruze rested his elbows back on the counter. "Yes. Who she is, where she is, I can't tell you. My wife, Estrellita, was not able to find out," he said. "Even though Olden Town and the Frisco Enclave are politically somewhat opposite, I don't believe in standing by and seeing all these men killed. I admire a woman with an interest in weaponry, something Estrellita unfortunately lacks, but still Lady Day seems to me mad and aimed against life." He hesitated, then added, "Should you find Penny, perhaps you could convince her to come back here. The silences here, the forest and the music. They should help her. Wouldn't you think?"

"I'll see what she thinks." Haley stood and left the weapon shop.

IV

A VERY OLD MAN in a wheelchair was being attacked by rooks and magpies on the broad lawn of the Nixon Institute as Haley rode up. The blue-black birds came spinning down from the red brick bell tower of the main building, darting and pecking at the old man's accessories. The old man had a tight two-handed grip on his silver acoustic guitar and he was batting at the diving birds. An unconscious rook popped up and landed near Haley's feet.

Parking his bike at the rack in front of the ballet school directly across the street from the institute, Haley crossed to the lawn and called out, "Shoo!"

"You birds are really dragging me down," said the old man, whose braided white beard was studded with fake gems. He clouted two more of the cawing birds, while a third nipped in and stole the false ruby from his belt buckle. "I know your thing is baubles, but you're making me all uptight, you know."

Haley trotted up and grasped the handlebars of the wheelchair. "Going inside?"

"Such was my intention," the old man said. "Then these birds started freaking around, you know. My baubles turn them on."

31

Haley noticed the word *Garbage* was spelled out in synthetic rhinestones on the old man's vest back. "You're here to be interviewed?"

"Right," he answered. "I'm a vital link with the cultural past of the United States. Recognize me, man?"

Haley started pushing the chair along the flagstone path to the entrance, sending the birds flickering up into the bright afternoon with his free hand. "No, I don't."

"Nat's Garbage Service," said the old man.

The grillework and glass doors hushed automatically open and Haley pushed the wheelchair up a slight ramp into a round, high domed lobby. "Pleased to meet you, Nat. My name is Haley."

"No, man. I'm not Nat. I'm Nat's Garbage Service. That is, I'm the only surviving member."

"A music group?"

"*The* music group," said the old man. "We got the Grammy in 1972. You wouldn't remember our big ones I guess. *Flowers Growing In The Cracks* and *Fragmented Syntaptic Authenticated Hallucinogenic Anthrax?*"

"No," said Haley.

"Lot of people, those who remember at all, think folk rock was a young people's music," said the old man. "Not so. I was thirty-seven before I got going, but I was turned on the right way. I was groovy in the right way, as it were. So I fit in."

"Oh, so." There was an arc shaped desk in the center of the cool dim room, a straight-backed Negro girl at the desk.

"At the height of it I had a hundred underage girls a day requesting plaster casts of my private parts," said the old man. "That was a fad then. I wonder where they all are now."

"The girls?"

"The plaster casts," the old man said. "It's depressing, man, thinking about it. Scattered in garbage pits, packed away in dusty rumpus rooms, maybe smashed." He rested his guitar on his sharp knees. "Man, I never thought I'd get sentimental. Old age is a puzzling thing."

The black girl smiled across at the old man. "Ten minutes late today, Mr. Pronzini."

"See, it all goes in cycles. Everybody is time-bound again." The old man propelled himself across the room and through a swinging door marked MUSIC ARCHIVES.

Haley moved to the desk. "I understand Penny Deacon was employed here," he said.

The girl smiled at him. "She is no longer."

"But she was?"

"You'll have to check with Personnel," said the receptionist. "That is, if you have some legitimate reason for your inquiry."

Haley showed her his PI Office credentials. "Where's Personnel?"

"I'm not through reading your IDs yet," smiled the black girl. "Um, um," she said to herself as she read. "Um, um, um." She nodded. "Okay. Personnel is usually up on Level 2 except that's being painted so they're in Reference & Retrieval. Door 6." She returned his credential pack and with the same sweep of her arm indicated the door. Her hand dropped and the forefinger jabbed a red button.

"What's that?"

"The Nixon Institute, which incorporates the Oral History Of The Then United States Project, is managed by the Parker Brothers. The Parkers have to know when anyone official is inside our Institute. They'll probably come down and shake your hand," she explained. "Protocol."

Haley responded to her latest smile with a quick bony grin and went through Door 6. A sloping corridor inclined toward another domed room. Portable computers, retrieval machines and hundreds of memory spools were stacked just inside the doorway. Banks of lights and grids walled the domed room.

"No, wait," a bald old man was saying to a mobile recording machine. "This was in 1969 or 70. Yes, 1970."

"Mrs. Silvermine," said the recorder, a squat gunmetal one, "don't tell me any more. You're in the wrong place. You're supposed to be up in Literature right now. Right this very minute."

"I'm not Mrs. Silvermine," corrected the old man. "That is, I am but that was merely a penname. Bertha M. Silvermine, the Queen of Spine-Tingling Horror. I was something in those days. You put up a poster in a drugstore or supermarket and all you had to say was, 'The latest Bertha M. Silvermine is here!' Wham. They'd break down the doors to buy the darned book. Bertha M. Silvermine was the Uncrowned Queen of the Gothics in those days. And I was writing that crap at the rate of three a month.

Three complete Bertha M. Silvermine novels a month. Those schmucks at the newsstands would barely recuperate from one assault by clamoring Bertha M. Silvermine fans when wham another novel would hit and here would descend the hordes of lonely old broads and untried maidens. But the contracts finally did me in. There was a slump in 1975, see? I finally had to start selling all rights. In 1976 some guy engraved one of my novels on the head of a pin. I didn't get one red cent. No, I'd sold head of a pin rights."

"Mrs. Silvermine," insisted the recording machine, "you took the wrong corridor. Please go to Literature. You're very late. If you don't get there it'll be your fanny in a sling."

"Fanny in a sling? What kind of sissy talk is that?" The old man whacked the lid of the recorder with a freckled fist.

"Well, that's as dirty as I'm programmed to get with old ladies."

"I'm not an old lady."

"Well, you go around calling yourself Bertha and you have to expect to cause confusion," the recorder said. "Now, listen. This is Reference & Retrieval and you're supposed to be in Literature."

The bald old author frowned over at Haley. "What's he getting at?"

"He's suggesting you're in the wrong area," said Haley. Except for the old man it was all machines in the R&R room.

"Oh, I'm glad you told me." The old man picked

a pair of gray gloves and a straw hat from atop the recorder and made his way into the corridor.

"What a dumb name, Bertha," said the recording machine.

"Where's Personnel?" asked Haley.

"Piled up in the corner."

"Who's in charge of it?"

"Nobody, all mechanized."

In the doorway two men cleared their throats. "Mr. Haley?" one of them inquired.

They were both tall and broad, both in their forties. One was dark and slightly roundshouldered, the other man light with his blond hair shaggy.

"Would you be the Parker Brothers?"

"Yes," said the dark one. "I'm F. Van Wyck Parker and this is my kid brother, Henry Nash Parker."

The blond man rubbed his nose with a thumb knuckle. "Look, Haley, what exactly are you prowling around for?"

His brother tapped his arm. "Calm, Hank. How can we help you, Mr. Haley?"

"I'm with the Private Inquiry Office," he told them. "I'm trying to locate a girl named Penny Deacon."

Henry Nash Parker rubbed at the tangled hair along his neck. "We're engaged in important work here at the Nixon Institute, Haley. People come nosing around and it screws up the oral history. Poking around, tracking mud on the floors and little bits of grass and bird feathers. It makes for a messy institute."

"Penny Deacon worked here," said Haley. "Can you tell me where she went?"

"I suppose," Henry Nash Parker went on, "you didn't see the door mat out there, Haley. Some detective you are. Big doormat that has Home Of The Oral History Of The Then United States embossed on it and you don't wipe your feet."

F. Van Wyck Parker, who had little round vinyl patches on the elbows of his work smock, said, "You'll have to excuse my kid brother, Mr. Haley. Old Mr. Nixon himself was in this morning and it got everyone pretty excited. Former Presidents of the United States are rare, as I needn't tell you."

"Everything went badly," said Henry. "Everything. Here we had a chance to record permanently the thoughts of this wonderful old fellow and it went badly. I knew it would from the moment the magpies stole the diamond out of his tie clasp."

"He's very old," said his brother. "You have to expect mishaps."

"All he'd say into our microphones," complained Henry, "was, 'I'm glad you asked me that question.' Christ, I get more out of that dumb Bertha M. Silvermine old fart."

"There'll be other interviews."

"Who wants to come back to a messy institute?" said Henry. "With mud clods and grass tracked all over the corridors."

The dark Parker Brother motioned to Haley. "You and I can talk upstairs, Mr. Haley. Stay here and unwind, Hank."

"Make him wipe his feet."

F. Van Wyck Parker led Haley to the corridor and then up a series of black metal spiral staircases. "You can imagine a project of the scope of ours is quite a strain. The kid brother lets it get him down now and then."

At the top of the final flight of steps they moved into the open air bell tower. The quiet buildings of San Anselmo far below now. "Okay," said Haley. "What can you tell me about Penny Duncan and where is she?"

"Wait," said the dark Parker. "Our late afternoon carillon is about to start."

When the automatic bells commenced playing, Parker rushed at Haley and began forcing him over the edge of the tower.

V

HANGING WITH his head upside down, halfway out of the high brick tower, Haley heard someone call, "Hold on, Haley." The bell tapes began playing *Hail To The Chief* and he couldn't hear what else was being shouted at him from down below on the bright lawns of the institute.

"Your respiration," grunted patch elbowed F. Van Wyck Parker, with a hand at Haley's throat, "will shortly cease to function."

Haley jabbed his elbows against the tower bricks

and thrust his body forward, bringing a knee into the oral historian's groin.

"Oof," said the Parker Brother. He made a brief anguished hopping and then got a fresh grip on Haley's throat. "What I'm using on you is *dofu*, a somewhat obscure form of Asiatic manual assassination. It emerged out of China at about the time of the Boxer Rebellion, the invention of a fanatic Malay physical culture professor."

Haley kneed him again. When Parker caught hold of Haley again and twisted his head far to the left the PI man got a look down. Coming up the outside of the brick tower, using suction tip grappling hooks, was a short bushy man. He had a curly moustache and was naked from the waist down.

"Kick him in the keaster," shouted the climbing man.

"Your comrade," gritted Parker, "also favors foul fighting. The advantage of dofu, which makes it difficult for the Occidental mind to accept is that it is remarkably clean. Fatal, but sportsmanlike."

Haley propelled himself forward once more, forcing Parker to let go and canter backwards. The two of them thunked into the bell tape console. The bells jumped ahead to the second chorus of *The Stars And Stripes Forever*.

"Why do you guys want to kill me?" asked Haley, jabbing at F. Van Wyck Parker's chin.

"You're on to us," said Parker. "You and that undressed scoundrel shinnying up our tower."

"Jump on his patootie." The partially dressed man leaped over the tower wall.

Haley sidestepped Parker's dofu lunge. "La Penna," he said, recognizing the newcomer as Joel La Penna of the Private Inquiry Office. "You're here?"

"Ganging up," said Parker. He dived around the console and jumped for the stairwell.

La Penna scratched his stomach just above the pubic hair. "Hi, Haley. Are you working on this case?"

Haley watched the last of Parker drop from view. "The Lady Day business?"

"No." La Penna shook his head. He had a dozen gray hairs at each temple, a gap between his two front teeth. "These Parkers are tied in with the Amateur Mafia."

"I read your reports in the PI office yesterday, but they didn't mention the Nixon Institute. You're working on the involuntary prostitution job."

"Right," said the PI agent. "I had a modeling school staked out here in San Anselmo, but then last night I got word these two brothers were selling girls on the side. I guess oral history and archives doesn't pay enough. Did you see the hangers on that receptionist downstairs, by the way?"

Haley grinned thoughtfully. "Thanks for saving me. Why don't you have any pants on, Joel?"

"I'm using that ballet academy across the road as an observation post," explained La Penna. "You know how ballet dancers are. Girl ballet dancers, I mean. I just happened to look up and notice you were being pushed out of the tower. 'Hey, that's Jim Haley getting tossed off the top of the Nixon Institute,' I said to Inga. It didn't mean anything to her. She just grabbed hold of my wang and said, 'So?' Most women today don't too much understand loyalty to a profession. You know why that is? Because a lot of guys are in lines of work they don't enjoy. You're lucky I put loyalty before screwing."

Haley crossed to the rim of the tower. "There go the Parker Brothers and the receptionist."

"Look at the way her keaster bounces when she runs," said La Penna, joining Haley.

"We better get trailing them. I have to find out where they put Penny Deacon."

"Penny Deacon? She's in San Rafael, working as a waitress in the Passtime Club."

"How'd you find that out?"

"She apparently got friendly with Inga while she was here. Inga got a vidphone call from her last night and she told her what she was up to. Nice looking girl, but too skinny for me. Not meaty enough for this hooker racket either, I'd guess. Restless, too." He thrust a pointing finger out. "Hey, that's Inga waving at us. Hi, Inga. Put your leotard back on, you dumb bimbo. Don't hang your equipment out the window like that. Look at those things jiggle."

Haley turned toward the stairs.

"Wait, Haley. Wave at Inga. Hey, Inga, you top heavy bimbo, this is my buddy, Haley."

"How many girls at the ballet school?" Haley started carefully down the stairs.

"Lord, over two dozen. And most of them live in. Last night they all tried to jump in the sack with me. I was busy trying to bug this institute, set up my observation gear. They keep clutching at my whacker. Ballet dancers. They're like that girl in the blue movie case. Remember that case?"

"Where you got all the extra evidence." The hallways of the Nixon Institute were cool and quiet. From far off, from around several turns drifted the voice of the old man who had been Bertha M. Silvermine.

"They kept wanting to reshoot the key scene," said La Penna. "Here I was posing as a blue movie actor. Sixteen takes on the orgy scene. I sort of liked the girl, but those damn chimpanzees got to be a bore."

"This Passtime Club. It's in that string of joints on B Street, isn't it?"

"Right, an Amateur Mafia joint. Hey, if you go there, be sure and get a look at the girl who pushes the pastry cart around. She's got an enlarged left buttock. Produces a weird effect when she walks. Her butt seems to go in and out of focus."

"You want to look for a pair of pants in the Parker closets?"

"No. Just to walk across the street?" The shaggy man shrugged. "You going on to San Rafael now?"

"Yes."

"Lady Day, huh? Getting worse, I hear."

"Getting more frequent. You know anything?"

"There's going to be a lot more guys killed, Haley," said La Penna. "Those Lady Day broads are mean. Obviously anybody who'd rather kill than screw is dangerous. I've picked up nothing specific, but I hear talk, scuttlebutt. Lady Day's going to keep at it. Unless somebody finds her and stops her."

"I'll get back to looking," said Haley.

VI

HALEY SWUNG off his bicycle and walked it to the toll gate. Twilight was darkening to night and as he approached the gate the toll man bent and flicked on the arch of lights over his gate. The man wore a police cap and a scarlet cloak. He was eating a meatball on a stick and flipping a metal half dollar. "Double or nothing?" he asked Haley.

Haley looked from the man to the electric letters above. *Welcome To San Rafael! If You Don't See It, Ask For It!* "No," Haley told him. He gave him fifty cents.

The toll man, whose fine wrinkles showed when the lights flashed orange, said, "This is San Rafael. You're getting off on the wrong foot."

"I don't like gambling," said Haley. "I came for the perversions."

The man took a sideways bite of his meatball. "Want to bet on how many times you'll make it tonight?"

"No fun if you keep score." Haley walked the bike through the toll gate, remounted and rode on.

Fanning out before him were long straight streets, lights fresh on. Words and promises glowed all around. *Uncle Tony's Dime Jig! Dance: $1, Love: $10; Freddie the Greaser's R Taco-Teria! Real Mex Food; Slum Village! 24 Kinds of Poverty Meals Now Being Served. We Never Close; Old-Fashioned Pop Tarts; Mother Columbia's Barrel House! Featuring the Winner and the Runners Up in the Miss Teen SFEnclave Pageant! Naked; Capt. Whackenjacker's Electronic Freak Shop; Fat Ed's Pastry Orgy! Eat All You Want! Babas au Rhum! Petitsfours! Swiss Meringue! Brownies! Plum Puddings! Danish; Marathon Bowling! Bowl Till You Drop; Gay Ralph's Authentic Fag Bar! Minors Welcome.*

Haley parked his bike in a rack in front of a robot pizzeria. Two broad men in peacoats were tussling with the bouncer in the vine draped doorway.

"Pucky," said one of the sailors. "I bet on anchovy and it came up anchovy."

"That's right," put in his companion. "We bet the robot chef would bake an anchovy pizza next."

"You bet on pepperoni," the husky bouncer insisted. "Look, if you boys are going to bet on the pizzas, you got to be prepared to lose. You ought to know the odds on pizza."

"Pucky," repeated the sailor.

The bouncer socked him twice on the chin and the sailor fell to the cracked sidewalk, spreading out slowly among the thrust up grass and weeds.

"Oh, what a mess," said his friend. "He's carrying an anchovy pizza under his coat." He raised a fist. "Why can't you be more careful, you dumb wop?"

"Dumb what?"

"Wop. Dago. You stupid dago."

44

The bouncer sighed. "You boys really are naive. Don't you really know who runs this place?"

"No," said the sailor. He dropped his fist, opened it. "You mean this is an Amateur Mafia operation?"

"This is an Amateur Mafia *town*," said the bouncer. "No Italians."

"Well, nice talking to you." The sailor walked away.

The bouncer dragged the unconscious sailor until he no longer blocked the entrance. He glanced over at Haley, nodded, made a chuckling sound. "Hi, Jim. See how I decked this one?"

"Efficient."

"Faster, too. My time is getting shaved down. If there was a speed record for cold cocking sailors I'd win a loving cup or something," said the big man. "You on business?"

"Partly. Where's Clem?"

"The boss? I think he's over at the Juke Box Arcade. Got time for a pizza?"

"No. Watch the bike, though."

The bouncer bent his knees slightly, squinted at the bike. "I notice you got a juju sign on the fender. Is that a nigger bike?"

Haley grinned a spare grin and walked down the block and into the Juke Box Arcade.

The rustic and sinewy old man who was the local Amateur Mafia chief said, "They shouldn't of done that, Jim." He rocked in his wicker rocker, his worn hands locked in his lap.

"A mutual misunderstanding, Clem," said Haley. "If I'd known the Parker Brothers were in with you

I would have just offered them some money for the information I wanted."

Clem Furrsy clicked his tongue against his slightly blue false teeth. "The Parkers ain't full time members of the Amateur Mafia, Jim. Merely affiliates. Our capo over in San Anselmo is sickly these days and sometimes he ain't as careful with screening as he could be." He rocked at a faster rate for a moment, reflective. "You got to be cautious with these book learning types. Got to look back into their geneology, too."

They were in a big one way glass booth in the very center of Clem Furrsy's Juke Box Arcade. Outside the booth a hundred antique juke boxes stood in circles. Each box played the top 100 tunes of a different year. About fifteen people were in the arcade now and the top tunes of a dozen different years blended. "Geneology?" asked Haley, perched on the edge of a wooden barrel.

"Something fancy like that. You know, where you find out what sort of people they had. You can't run a good criminal organization without being selective." He laughed, reached into the bib pocket of his overalls. "I plumb forgot, Jim, you're on the other side. Law and order. I'll tell you for true, Jim, that there Private I outfit of yours would look a lot sharper if you had started it off on a more selective basis." He slid a harmonica out of the pocket and blew into it once. "Turn off that monitor mike, will you? She-it, but I hate that noise out there."

Haley flicked a toggle switch on the bank of them mounted on the pot bellied stove. He said, "I'd like to avoid any more assassination attempts. While I'm in San Rafael, Clem."

"Nobody's laid a hand on you yet, Jim," said Furrsy. "Course, you would of been wiser not to come riding in on a jigaboo bicycle. Know what I mean?" He blew a few notes of *Old Dan Tucker*.

Haley's grin was still brief and thin. "I'm here on something that has nothing to do with the AM."

Furrsy left off playing. "Don't be too sure, Jim. We got our fingers into a lot of pies. We got more rackets than a sow has tits."

"How much are you charging for safe conduct these days, Clem?"

"I wished to goodness it was free, Jim. Cause you're a real nice young fellow. You got a pretty good geneology, too." He whapped the harmonica on his knee to free it of saliva. "A hundred bucks."

"A hundred? I'm not moving in, Clem. I'll only be here till about midnight."

"She-it. I'm charging you a third off list price as it is," said the Amateur Mafia leader. "I tell you honest, Jim, some of the younger fellows would like to sock you for $200 or more. They just flat don't care for the PI Office much. And I bet you can't guess why?"

"Because we have Italians." Haley got out his wallet and took a hundred dollars in tens out.

Returning the harmonica to its place, Furrsy drew out a six inch length of tree branch. "Well, that's right clever of you. You done guessed it first crack." He found a jackknife on a nearby stool top, unclasped it and began whittling. "This here's an alder branch."

"It's crab apple."

"No she-it? I should of knowed that. My folks are outdoor people three generations back." He reached out with the knife-holding hand and got the money, grunting at the far end of the reach. "Yep, you got all them wops in PI. Specially that randy one, La Penna. How's he doing?"

"Last time I saw him he was walking into a girls' ballet school without his pants."

"That's La Penna sure enough," laughed Furrsy. "Course most all them dagos are goofy about sex." He leaned back in his old rocker, ticked his chin with the one leaf left on the twig. "You take this here now Mafia them wops started. Basically, down at the ground level of it, that was a danged good idea. Still good, ain't it? What they sometimes call organized crime. Now if one of your major races had of thought of the Mafia first, why things wouldn't be in the sorry shape they are nowadays. A good god-fearing white protestant Mafia could have held the United States together. You bet your ass. Well, now, better late than never. We got the Amateur Mafia going now, got organized crime in the hands of a better class of people. I tell you, Jim, things ain't going to collapse as much any more. They might perk up even."

"You'll put out the word?" said Haley. "That I can come and go in your town."

"Sure thing," said Furrsy. He took a swipe at the twig with his blade. He still had the money in his palm, wadded. "What you on to anyhow, Jim?"

"Lady Day."

A lock of Furrsy's white hair dropped over his forehead. "She-it! Don't up and tell me I got Lady Day people right here in San Rafael."

"No," said Haley. "Just somebody who wants to sell some information. Not anybody in your organization, Clem."

"Better not be," said Furrsy. "Well, you done paid up and you got yourself six hours to roam around free as a bird."

"Don't have one of your guys tail me this time," suggested Haley.

"Nope, won't," said Furrsy. "But she-it oh dear, Jim, riding around on a nigger bicycle, you're bound to stand out like a sore thumb."

When Haley got outside he found the controversial bike had been stolen. He walked on, shaking Furrsy's tail in under ten minutes.

VII

A PLUMP WOMAN in a blue leather shift was scratching her elbow in front of the Passtime Club. Her escort, a short frail man with a vinyl toupee, kept reaching up and running his finger around the lace collar of the woman's dress. "Come on, come on," he said. "Come on, Mae."

"I can't decide," she said.

Haley stopped a few feet from them.

The doorman said to the plump woman, "I bet you have an impressive figure, lady. Why not abandon caution, which would be in keeping with the spirit of San Rafael in general and the Passtime Club in particular, and disrobe yourself?"

"Come on, come on, Mae," said the little man with the plastic hair. "Here, look. I'm doing it, too." He unfastened his plaid ascot.

"Inside for that," warned the doorman. "No stripping down on the sidewalk. They got an ordinance."

"I was only offering encouragement."

"Tell me the prices again," requested Mae.

"Five bucks each if you want to come in clothed. Two bucks each if you strip and frequent the Passtime naked."

"Come on, Mae. We'll save six bucks."

"A lot of our more mature customers appreciate a full-bodied woman, lady." the doorman assured her. "You'll get lots of admiring glances, and probably a few free drinks."

"I don't know," said Mae. "Will anybody try to fondle me or pinch me?"

"No, no. We don't allow rough stuff."

"We really only came to hear the big band here," said Mae.

"You can hear them just as good with your clothes off, Mae, and we save six bucks."

"Well, so long as I don't get pinched. All right."

"Good," said the doorman. "Four bucks, buddy. Plus a buck gratuity."

After the couple paid and entered Haley walked over to the doorway. "One," he said and gave the doorman an Edward R. Murrow five dollar bill.

"Only two bucks if you plan to strip down."

"No. I came for the music."

"Who'd have thought swing would have a rebirth in the waning years of the 20th Century," said the doorman. "I minored in swing at college—did a thesis on Jimmie Lunceford. Culture is an amazing thing, isn't it, the patterns?"

Haley grinned. "Is Penny Duncan working now?"

"Information is $10 per item, buddy."

Haley gave him a second piece of money. "Okay."

"You'll find her," said the doorman, after flicking the bill into a braid trimmed pocket of his military cut leotard, "in our Smorgasbord Room. Her shift is 4:00 P.M. to 10:00 P.M. For a dollar more I'll give you a warning."

"Throw it in free." Haley put a palm against the padded door.

"Very well, since you're a swing enthusiast. I noticed the flicker of recognition in your eyes when I mentioned the Lunceford band. Who was Trummy Young?"

"Played trombone with his feet," said Haley. "Now about the free warning."

"This Penny Deacon is pretty thick with our bandleader, even though she's only been here a short while." He poked a photo poster taped to the whitewashed stone wall above his head. "He's the one with the moustache and the saxophone. Hobart 'Big Mac' MacGregor. Not a bad alto man for an ofay, but he's got a mean streak. Careful he doesn't cut you up."

"Thanks." Haley grinned quickly and pushed inside.

Mae was only half out of her clothes just in front of the check room. Her escort, frail and naked, was trying to snap his fingers, while he said, "Come on, Mae. Get a move on. The next set is about to start."

"Undressing in public," said Mae, "I'm not used to."

"It's always tough the first time, kiddo," said the naked check girl. A chubby blonde. "Don't let skeleton dance there bother you."

The interior of the club simulated a series of connecting caves. The thin light was blue tinted. About half the fifty customers in the nearest cavern were naked. A nude host caught Haley's arm and smiled. "A table, sir?"

"Which way for the smorgasbord?"

The host said, "Cavern C, through that tunnel on your far left. Don't you want to hear the swing, though?"

"Can't I hear it in C?"

"Well, yes, some. But you miss the showmanship. Look there."

Blue velvet curtains parted in the far wall of this cave and a nude man with a trombone emerged. He strutted toward the bandstand, with the horn bell aimed at the room's rocky ceiling.

"*South Rampart Street Parade*," explained the host. "A classic from swing's golden era."

A naked trumpeter marched in after the trombonist. His horn aimed at the floor. He flapped a tiny gold derby over the trumpet mouth. After several more horns marched in, the rhythm section entered. The piano last, pushed by a set of naked red-haired girl twins. The piano player was stretched out on top of the instrument, playing it by reaching down to the keys.

"That's a real tricky thing," said the host. "He has to play the bass part with his right hand. It's something like trying to rub your head while patting your stomach."

"Is he going to do that, too?"

"No."

"I won't wait, then." Haley cut around the edge of the cave while the musicians were strutting and marching up a ramp to the stage. A single silver spotlight popped on and revealed a naked alto saxophone player being lowered from the ceiling in a gondola shaped like a half moon. "Ladies and gentlemen," announced a hidden loudspeaker, "Big Mac MacGregor, the new king of swing." The bandleader looked to be about twenty pounds overweight.

Cavern C was a dim yellowish green. Haley was five steps across its gravelly floor when a handful of garbanzo beans hit him in the eye. "Easy now," he said.

There were only four other people in the room, all of them grouped around a sparsely stocked smorgasbord table. Haley got a vague impression of the man in the peacoat who'd thrown the garnish at him. He noticed first the girl behind the table. She was wearing a short candy striped kimono, leaning slightly forward. Her dark hair was worn long. She was slender, tanned. The lines of her high cheek bones and the faint hollows beneath her eyes were smoke colored. She was pretty, but not in any traditional way. There was an unexpected, brand new quality about her.

The man in the peacoat grabbed a handful of sweet pickles and threw them at the naked, tatooed bouncer. "Pucky," he said.

The bouncer again ducked and the pickles sailed toward Haley. This time Haley dodged, moving on into the cavern and toward the girl.

"Okay," growled the bouncer. "We'll make it ten. Ten is what I'm going to count and then you two bozos better leave."

The two men were the sailors who had been arguing over the pizza. The second one was stripped down to a suit of raveled thermal underwear. "Oh, yeah," he said. "We'll smack a damage suit on you, Amateur Mafia or not."

"No, no," said his partner. "We don't want any trouble with the AM. All we ask is what's right and just."

"Look, bozos," said the bartender. "You guys got to order the full smorgasbord dinner for two before you get naked waitresses during the slack hours. That's the rules."

"But a smorgasbord dinner for two shouldn't cost fifty bucks."

"It's the *complete* smorgasbord, bozo."

"Yeah, well, we been around, to most of the ports in what's left of the four corners of the world," said the sailor in the underwear. "And we never got socked for no $50 for smorgasbord. Not even in Port Said."

"This is San Rafael," said the bouncer. "And that's the price. If you bozos can't come up with it, get off the turf."

Haley stopped across from the girl. "Good evening," he said, grinning.

Her brown eyes widened slightly, then she smiled a wide quirky smile at him. "You've got olive oil all over you. Here." She held out one long fingered hand and dabbed at his face with a pastel handkerchief. She couldn't quite reach. "No, that's no good. You'll fall in the potato salad if you lean anymore." She ducked down and went under the table, emerging long legs first on his side of it. "Now then."

Haley continued to grin as she wiped his face and then his jacket. Finally he said, "Thanks."

"You grin a hell of a lot," the girl said. "Even when people throw things at you."

"It's a reflex."

"I don't know. Maybe you just see things in a particular way."

The dressed sailor said, "We've been pushed around too much in this rattletrap town. We're up in arms."

"I was born and raised here," said the bouncer, who had a dolphin tattooed on his left bicep. "I don't take to your calling this a rattletrap town, bozo."

"Pucky." The other sailor crunched a French roll on the bouncer's thin haired head.

"The specialty of the house," said the girl. "I've

been here two nights and we haven't sold one complete smorgasbord yet."

"Probably a good thing."

"Oh, I don't mind undressing," said the girl. "That's the easiest part." She touched absently at the bow tied belt of the kimono. "Look, for $10 you can buy me a drink at one of those tables against the wall. Or just sit. Would you?"

"Sure," said Haley. As they walked across the cavern the bouncer pushed the dressed sailor back over into the decorative suckling pig. "I'm Jim Haley," Haley said to the girl.

"Okay." She took the wall side of the table and nodded him down opposite her. From the other cavern came the strains of *Clap Hands, Here Comes Charlie.* "Nobody will bring us anything till this set is over. My name is Penny Deacon. Oh, you better put $10 on the table top in case the management does look in."

Haley did. "Okay, done."

"You have a basically honest face," said Penny. "It's a little too bony, but even the bones look honest. You ever hear of an oldtime actor named James Coburn?"

"No."

"He had a bony but honest face, too. But nothing at all like yours," said the girl. "I had an uncle who was a movie freak. This was down in the Republic. That's all gone down, all to pieces now. Everybody has different important dates, which is why history is so hard to share. For a lot of people I guess Southern California went to pieces way back during the war, the invasion. With us it was only three and some years ago." She stopped, smiled her quirky smile. "Very verbal. First time in weeks. Your turn. Say something bony and honest."

Haley said, "I'm an operative for the Private Inquiry Office and I want you to help me locate Lady Day."

Penny put her arms up on the table, hugged her elbows. "Not that honest," she said. "That's from an old joke. Not that shaggy. I had another uncle who was a joke collector. People are always collecting things around me. Like the floating saxophonist out there."

"And he's collecting you."

Penny nodded. "He assumes he is, at the moment. See, I now and then get the idea I need somebody to lean on. A popular delusion and madness of the crowd. Big Mac. Big Mac looked like he might be helpful. I was in one of my periodic prop-me-up moods when I started working here. I don't know." She paused and watched him. "What kind of deal?"

"What do you want?"

She smiled. "That's too specific. Right at the moment, though, I think this place is even less interesting than the Nixon Institute. I worked there."

"I know."

"Sure, that's right. You're almost a cop," said Penny. "You have a big file on me, stuffed in a data box or someplace?"

"Not me, no," said Haley. "I can get you safely out of here, if that's what you want. Get you probably a thousand bucks for providing me with information. Depends on the information."

"I act on impulse a lot," said Penny. "You'll find that out. Right now I'm in the mood to go along with you. I'll need, maybe, some protection. Lady Day, that outfit, they're tough. Nobody tougher than a . . ."

"Than what?"

"Nothing. They're likely to try to do me in if I give you information. One of the few charms of this job is I have the AM to stand between me and any assaults."

"Nobody's going to get a chance to hurt you, Penny."

"That'll be a switch," said the girl. "Okay, Jim. I guess it's a deal. My shift here is until ten. I'll have a better chance of slipping away if I do it at the usual time. Big Mac and his magic saxophone thinks I'm going to spend the night with him again. I guess the two of us can help him shake that notion. I'll meet you at the rear entrance, off the parking lot at ten. Okay?"

"Yeah," said Haley. "Do you know where Lady Day is? Who she is?"

"No," said Penny. "Not exactly. What I can sell you is the location of one of her recruiters. It's how I got involved. I guess my other uncle is the one who brought you in on this. The old arrowsmith?"

"Yes. This recruiter, is she in town here?"

Penny shook her head. "It's a guy, more or less, and he's down the coast in a town called San Arturo. You know it?"

"Inland, between Frisco and Carmel."

"That's the place," said Penny. "I won't tell you any more details now. I'll go along to the town with you. I guess I'm in the mood for an excursion. Will that be okay?"

Haley told her it would.

The two sailors were still confronting the bouncer when Haley left the cavern. Something crashed among them, but Haley didn't see what. When he looked back over his shoulder it was to grin at Penny.

VIII

HALEY CHOSE a booth at the end of an outdoor cluster of public vidphone booths and called the Intelligence and Investigation Office. After several buzzes and a droning, Chief McGuinness showed on the sticky circle screen.

"Hello, Jim. Why are you waving at me?"

"I'm wiping chile gravy off the viewer."

The big slumped chief of intelligence was half into a broad ribbed cardigan. "I'm at home. They switched your call. You haven't seen our place since Tildy got the bear baiting posters up, have you?"

"That's right," said Haley. "I want some background files. See what you have and I'll check back in an hour."

"Wait, are you . . . where? Gravy on the screen, must be San Rafael. The trail led you there?"

"Yes."

"I can videofax some information to you. We have an agent there who has a v-fax."

Haley said, finally, "Okay. I want what you can get on Penny Deacon and Hobart 'Big Mac' MacGregor."

"That's the mysterious girl, is it? Penny Deacon." McGuinness had the sweater all the way on and was scribbling on the edge of a punch card. "What's she look like?"

Elbows were bumping into walls two booths over. Haley said, "Five feet seven, about 120 pounds, dark brown hair, faintly freckled, small star shaped scar just above left knee, pretty, high cheek bones, nice outdoor tan."

"That's very thorough."

"She wasn't very dressed when I met her."

McGuinness blinked. "You're not turning into another La Penna?"

"No. A lot of people are undressed around here. It's a fad." Two booths over, three underage boys and two twenty year old Negro girls were undressing and wriggling. "Here's what Big Mac MacGregor looks like." Haley described the saxophone player.

McGuinness shook his head twice. "Where are you calling from?"

"Public booth."

"I hear grunting sounds in the background."

"Some people are grappling near here," explained Haley. "Who's the guy with the v-fax machine?"

"His name is Claypoole. He runs the San Rafael Social Relief Center on D Street. I'll shoot what I can find over to him." McGuinness' head clicked up. "Is that somebody naked behind you?"

Haley turned. "Yes, it is. I'll see you later." He cut off.

On the buckled mosaic tile in front of his booth a young girl was tugging off her lemon yellow underwear. It had the name Pearline embroidered all over it. "We're trying for the record again," the pale girl told Haley.

"What record, Pearline?"

"I'm not Pearline. This is just her skimpies. I slipped them on by mistake after our last record attempt." She paused, took a breath. "The naked phone booth record. We've got a call in now." She dropped her underwear at his feet and pointed at the crowding booth.

Seven naked young people were in there now. A black girl in a floating foetal position. "That's right," she was saying. "We want KENC-TV in Frisco. You know, the television station with the Dick Reisberson Show on it. You know Dick Reisberson. I don't know if he's a newscaster. No, I'm talking about the Dick Reisberson who has the naked phone booth contest going on."

Haley left the area.

A metal plaque on the brown wood face of the welfare store explained in 12 point type: *Charity is more than a handout. It is a means of communication, a sympathetic rapport. Thus physical ambiance is as important as psychological attitude. Thus each Social Relief Center is designed to make you feel at home. This WS was built in 1993 by the Joint S.F. Enclave/San Rafael Relief Center Committee and is based on the type of general store current in the then United States in 1890, which was in the last century.*

Under this someone had scratched: *Claypoole is a sissy.*

Haley entered the narrow store and the bell suspended over the wood and glass door tinkled.

"Sit on the bench and take a form," ordered the cracker barrel on his immediate left.

"I'm not here for food," said Haley. "I have business with Claypoole."

"Sit on the bench and take a form," repeated the yellow barrel. Its speaker grid was loose and buzzed when it spoke.

"He can't say nothing else," said a frail old man who was on the bench with a form in his hand. "He's one way. Long as you stand in his vicinity he'll keep on saying that same darn thing."

Haley extracted a pink form from the top of the barrel and crossed the swayed wood floor. "Know where Claypoole's office is?"

"Back of the counter. But Uncle Dave'll knock you on your duff if you try to go in there. About the only thing Claypoole'll come into the store proper for is a protest and that takes fifty people."

"Who's Uncle Dave?"

The old man pointed through the musty dimness. "The store proprietor, a mean old andy."

Up from behind a tall jar of saltines appeared a

cherubic android, pink faced with spectacles, corn cob pipe, tossled white hair. "Howdy, stranger. Got your food coupons all in order?"

The old man whispered, "He's a stubborn old cuss. He still insists we're on coupons, even though we been on script for two years or more now. Haven't we?"

Haley nodded, moved closer to the android. "I want to see Claypoole. Tell him Haley."

The pink old machine chuckled. "Now, why should I go up to a feller and say Haley? Don't make much sense." He sucked his pipe stem and exhaled smoke. "You disabled or what?"

"I'm Haley. To see Claypoole on S.F. Enclave business."

"Pretty sassy for a cripple, if you are," said the android. He sidestepped and leaned in the direction of the sitting old man. "Hey, you old coot. Are you still puzzling over that questionnaire?"

"I forget how to spell malnutrition." He fluttered the form. "Over here in the List Six Things You Are Probably Suffering From part."

"We might waive that portion if you hurry up and fill in the rest."

"What's the handout tonight anyway?"

"Kid vitamins."

"What? To restore my youth?"

"No, you ninny. These here are surplus children's multiple vitamins in the form of animal shaped candy."

"What animals?"

"Dogs, apes, elephants, chipmunks, bullfrogs, gazelles, lemurs and tarsiers."

The old man smacked his lips half-heartedly. "I guess it's better than starving."

Haley leaped over the counter. He landed in front of the wood door marked CLAYPOOLE/DIRECTOR and tapped on it with a knobby fist.

"Hey, feller," cried Uncle Dave, clutching up a wooden headed mallet.

The door inched inward and a pale Negro stared out. "Don't put the clout on him, Uncle Dave. He's okay."

"Come jumping over my counter like a hyena," complained the android. "Talked back to the cracker barrel, pretended to be a hopeless cripple. More than likely conspired to stage a protest." He clunked a hanging cheese with his mallet.

"Come in, Mr. Haley," said Claypoole, beckoning.

Haley, once inside the small vastly clean office, asked, "You got the material from I&I?"

Claypoole stroked the tip of his nose with two fingers. "We have to be both firm and somewhat arbitrary with the people who frequent us. You can understand that?"

Haley said, "What did McGuinness send?"

Claypoole sighed. "This double life is a burden. I don't know if you're familiar with the rural blues song that contains the lines, 'Early this morning my blues came tumbling down. I was all locked up, lord, and prisoner bound' . . . ?"

"No."

"That's how I feel quite often." Claypoole picked several sheets of flimsy fax paper from his small desk.

"You picking up anything on Lady Day here?" Haley asked as the Negro handed the sheets across.

"No," said Claypoole. "I'm not up on *everything* in the world with a touch of negritude in it, after all."

Haley leafed through the pages. "This is all?"

"That's it, yes," said Claypoole. "Not too much on either of them. Although what there is on that Deacon girl is quite interesting. A pretty complex biography to accompany one so relatively young, isn't it?"

Haley tucked the sheets into an inside pocket and did not reply.

IX

HALEY SAID, "I want to rent a land car."

The short, dark, balding man was standing with legs wide, surrounded by a hundred used vehicles. "Take the damn Surprise Coins first. We're playing the Surprise Coin Bank Night History Game this week and I want to hand out a hundred of these little dingbats every day."

Haley let the man drop the coins in his palm.

They were big and gilt and showed famous assassinations of the past. "Hey, aren't you . . . ?"

"Bruce Carter," said the small man quickly. He pointed at the car lot's several colored light displays of his name for verification.

"You've had your nose changed," said Haley. "But you're Bruno Calimari."

"Quiet, Haley. Button your lip. Don't be a fink on me," cautioned the dark man. "This burg is up to here in Amateur Mafia torpedoes."

"This isn't a Mafia town, no," agreed Haley. "Why are you here, Bruno?"

Calimari jiggled the eighty historic coins left in his jumpsuit pockets. "You always was straight with me, Haley, even though me and you are on different sides of what's left of the law. You work your side of the street, I work mine. Once in awhile you've laid a handful of finifs on me, a couple yards of kale. You scratch my back, I scratch yours."

"Okay, so what's going on?"

"I'm an undercover agent. Get me?"

"Sure, but why?"

Calimari said, "You really want a car, Haley? I got a couple aren't hot or lemons. I wouldn't want to stick you with a clunk. Get me?"

"I really have use for a car."

"I can let you have that green one over there," said Calimari. "You going to be out of this burg by nine tonight?" He wandered to the green land car.

"Well, no." Haley kicked at the car's synthetic tires.

"Just so you ain't going to be on B Street."

"I will be on B Street, Bruno. Sometime after nine. What's coming up?" Haley placed his hand alongside his wallet. "Have you got some information to sell?"

Bruno puckered his mouth. "I ain't angling for no cumshaw, Haley. You're an on the level guy, a heads up eye. Get me? So I'm going to level with you, give you a free tip." He knelt beside the used land car and when Haley was squatting beside him on the pastel asphalt, Bruno continued. "See we're still pretty old country in the Mafia. We're the real Mafia, after all, and got a tradition to uphold. But we also can keep up with what's going on. Lately we been studying—now don't give me the horse laugh, Haley—we been studying about guerrilla warfare. You heard of that?"

"Yes. You're planning some kind of terrorist raid on B Street tonight, against the Amateur Mafia joints?"

Bruno laughed. "You always was a double dome, Haley. You guessed it. Yeah, and I'll tell you this urban guerrilla stuff—we read about it in some chink books—it turns out to be not too different from the way we used to operate in the old days. Lots of shooting, element of surprise. The lay is this. We're going to hit B Street right smack at nine tonight and give it the works. Get me? I don't like to see you be a fall guy and get caught there. So my advice is you should stay clear."

"Nine?"

Bruno said, "Nine on the nose. We got stop watches."

"Well, she'll have to quit an hour early tonight," Haley said. "I imagine you're including the Passtime Club on your raid?"

"You bet. Going to toss a pineapple in there."

"Wait," Haley told him. "No bombs."

"How come you say no bombs?"

"I'm going to be inside the Passtime. I was planning on going there at ten, but now it'll have to be earlier." He looked up at one of the lot clocks. "It's nearly eight now."

"I don't know, Haley. I'd like to help you out."

"Shooting outside is okay, and noise. It's a diversion."

"Sure, they talk about them in the chink books."

Haley stood. "I'll take the car, for a week. Pay in advance?"

"No, I trust you. Going out of this immediate area?"

"Maybe."

"I'll give you a list of the other Bruce Carter lots and you can turn it in at any of them. See, I got a legit business on top of my undercover work. Make you a price of $20 a day and fuel free."

"Sold," said Haley. "Who's going to be driving on your raid tonight?"

Bruno was still half crouching. "The Macri brothers and Little Nick Caporizzi."

"The Macris know me," said Haley. "Ask them as a favor, no bombs."

"I'll try," said Bruno.

Haley hurried along the rocky corridor. A saxophone solo suddenly stopped behind a nearby, half open door.

"You're sure a bitch tonight," said a man with a nasal voice.

"I always am," said Penny. "It just took you this long to notice, Mac."

"A lot," said Big Mac, "a lot of broads think being serenaded by the leading sax, the leading alto sax man, in the Frisco area is pretty romantic."

"I doubt the women you impress know an alto from a tenor."

"You care very little for me and my talent, Penny," complained the Passtime orchestra leader. "This version of *Body and Soul* you've been yawning through I copied note for note from a famous Coleman Hawkins solo on a real old record."

"Since you're neither Hawkins nor a saxophone," said the girl, "what difference does it make?"

"You're a dialectic bitch," said Big Mac. "It was a different story last night."

"You didn't bring the saxophone to bed."

Big Mac said, "Damn you, Penny. Stop kidding around with me. You don't recognize an authentic emotion when you see it."

"I don't know. Whistle a little of it."

Haley entered Big Mac's dressing room. "Hello, Penny. For good and valid reasons we have to leave ahead of schedule."

"How'd you get here, pal?" Big Mac MacGregor rose from a rattan love seat and slammed his saxophone carefully down on a tufted hassock beside him.

"I bribed a couple of people."

"Yeah, well," Big Mac said, getting his shaggy synthetic camel's hair bathrobe back on, "I'm going to get the bouncer to toss you out on your can, pal."

"He's one of the guys I bribed." Haley grinned across the purple tinted room at Penny. She was still wearing her candy striped kimono, but her hair was up, tied with a scarlet ribbon. "Get your things together, Penny."

"Okay." She moved from the folding chair she'd been on.

"What's going on here?" asked Big Mac. "I smell a conspiracy." He jammed his puffy freckled hands into his robe pockets.

"Watch out," Penny warned Haley.

Big Mac's right fist came out clutching a paring knife. "Shut up, bitch. I'm going to fix this guy and then maybe I'll do a little something for you."

Haley eased closer to the man. "Get collected, Penny. Meet me in the corridor."

She moved quietly to the doorway.

"Now, pal," said Big Mac, and lunged.

Haley hopped backwards, over the saxophone and hassock. Big Mac went straight-arming by. Haley jumped again and caught the flying skirts of the robe. His big knobby fingers gripped it and he jerked. Big Mac was yanked off course, began side stepping wildly. He cracked into the simulated stone wall. Haley was there now and he chopped the knife from his hand. He punched three jabs to Big Mac's lowering chin. The robe ballooned up, hit the floor several seconds after Big Mac, settled on his stretched out body in slow wavering folds.

Haley crossed to the door, stepped into the dim corridor, closed the door. From a distance came the sound of gunfire.

Penny came from around a bend, a small canvas suitcase in her hand. She was wearing a sleeveless sweater, tan slacks. "Is that why we're leaving ahead of time?"

He nodded. "It's the real Mafia, two minutes early."

"Come on." She pointed at a red exit door. "You knew they were coming?"

Haley's shoulder hit the heavy door and it opened onto the night. "Yes."

"You didn't warn anybody but me."

He caught her bare arm and led her to his rented land car. "That's right."

Penny got in and hooked up the seat straps while Haley put himself at the driving panel. As he pushed the start button the girl said, "So now you know, from walking in on Big Mac, a little more about me. And I know a little more about you."

Haley drove the car across the parking area and away from the shooting and yelling of B Street. He looked once over at Penny. He grinned, but did not reply.

There was a large explosion behind them and glass and plastic words and names rose, fragmenting, into the clear dark sky.

X

THE COAST highway snapped and undulated and an enormous plastic hamburger fell in their path. Haley swerved. The land car bucketed off the road and across a grass and gravel field. Another and deeper earthquake rolled and the big wooden Fat Ed swayed and quivered atop the blacked out drive-in. Plastic onion rings somersaulted from the plate in his giant hand, drifted and spun down through the faint mist. One ring slapped against the front window of the car. Haley braked and the machine bumped gently into an overgrown willow tree and stopped.

"Christ," said Penny. She unbuckled herself and reached for Haley. Her arms went around him and she held tight.

"Easy now," he said.

Fat Ed made a ripping splintering sound and went over backwards, feet up. The twenty foot high wooden boy landed on his head in the back lot of the old drive-in. He flipped over again, smashed through a retaining fence and went sledding down the bushy hillside toward the dark ocean below.

"It's not going to stop," said Penny. Her head pressed against his chest hard. "We're all going to fall off the edge of the world."

"No," said Haley. He got the fingers of one bony hand tangled in her hair, twisted in the scarlet ribbon. He eventually stroked her hair, with a soothing motion. "A bad run of quakes. But they seem to be getting less."

"I can't ever get used to quakes," said Penny, still holding on. "That's funny, because I've gotten used to most everything else you can think of."

Haley said, "It's okay." The earth was calm now and no more rumblings came. He stroked his hand along the girl's arm.

Her head still against him, Penny said, "You're lucky I didn't call you Dad. Times at night if there's a quake or something that frightens me, I call him. I think whoever I'm with is him. He was a pretty average, not exceptional man. But I had the impression he could do almost anything. Then they killed him, just like that, in a minute. Quick just like that. It really surprised me a lot." She looked up at Haley now. "Earthquakes make me sentimental. I'm sorry." She gave him a brief smile.

Haley bent and kissed her.

Penny said, "I'd like you now, Jim. Now, here." She hooked her arms around his neck, then let go and smiled. "Oh, but you're still all strapped to the seat."

"We'll remedy that," Haley said.

Face up, Fat Ed was bobbing at the edge of the Pacific Ocean, white foam sizzling around his wooden head.

"Poor Fat Ed," said Penny, walking barefoot

around him on the sand. "I'm sure your parents had higher hopes for you. Fat Ed, Sr. and Mrs. Fat Ed, Sr. College certainly, some kind of business career. 'But, Fat Ed, Sr., our boy is, you know, very tall. Exceptionally tall.' 'Shut up, Mrs. Fat Ed, Sr., everybody has a handicap of some sort in this world. Don't pamper him. He's got his row to hoe. Even with the world falling apart, there's plenty of jobs for anyone willing to work.' 'But, Dad, I got my heart set on show business. I want to stand on top of a hamburger stand on the Pacific Coast Highway.' " The girl walked back over the sand to where Haley was sitting on a driftwood log. "Hi."

Haley grinned, nodded.

Penny took a place beside him. "I have a son, someplace. Some bureau or other has him placed somewhere. Four years old. Did you know that?"

"Yes."

"You've been reading up on me?"

"I was given some . . ." he began. "Never mind. I can't think of any word that doesn't sound like business."

"Data, info, input, backgrounding, fill in," said the girl. "Scuttlebutt. Pick one."

"Scuttlebutt sounds okay."

Penny said, "Well, nobody knows that much about me. Not even the police or your Intelligence people. I was an only child and I've felt sort of private and mysterious ever since. "

Haley rested a hand on her back. "Penny, I have to keep on with this Lady Day business."

"What else? If everybody I slept with dropped

everything to concentrate on me, by now California, both halves, would be at a standstill." She turned toward him and he looked away to the dark ocean. "You're still sentimental a little, Jim. You'd like me to be something I'm not."

"No," he said. "Right now I've only known you half a day. I don't even know for sure who you are. When I do, that's enough. I won't tell you who I think you should be. I like you, Penny. I want to keep with you, for awhile."

"Okay. You're slightly humoring me maybe," she said. "Because I've told you, and you can also probably guess it just by taking a good look, that I don't want to stop or sit still anymore. So because we've made love, and will again, that's nothing momentous. That won't make the earth shake and knock fat boys into the sea. Okay?"

Haley said, "Well, that's a good enough tentative way to approach us. So stop for now."

Her fingertips reached up and touched his face. "I saw the grin. All right, you can be mysterious, too. We'll spend a few days together anyway, see what happens." She stood and paced away from him. "When we get to San Arturo the guy you want to watch is a faggot named Buddy Plastino."

Haley shifted from the log to the sand, stretched some, hunkered down a bit. He interlocked his hands behind his head and watched the girl and the ocean beyond her. "Tell me tomorrow," he said.

XI

FLAT YELLOW FIELDS, wire and stump fences and low gnarled trees surrounded the town of San Arturo. A ten year old hopper was skimming the field at their far left, crop dusting.

Fenny tapped with two fingers on the scuffed buckles of her seat straps. First the buckle under her left breast, then the one on her left hip. She reached out and touched Haley's cheek.

He gave her a pleased, modified grin. "Yes?"

"I still like you. I was affirming it," said the slim pretty girl. "The trouble is, you're probably too substantial."

"Still, the time is piling up. We've been together now almost a day."

"You grin like the Shropshire cat." She hugged herself.

"You're thinking of the Cheshire lad." Haley slowed the land car as they entered the low narrow town.

"Still and all," she said, "the basic reason we're together is because you have a specific job and I'm somebody who's tangled up in the works. The best hotel is two blocks up on our right, but drive around some first and I'll point out landmarks."

There were only a few blocks of San Arturo. The buildings were low, many of adobe, some stucco fronted, a few frosted with Victorian gingerbread. "This Buddy Plastino runs a playhouse here?" asked Haley.

"Yes, he's the actor-manager and a noted tourist attraction," answered the girl. "Keep driving up this way and then turn right after the hotel. Yes, Buddy calls his playhouse the New Punch And Judy Theater. His specialty is anti-female plays. That's a fairly popular genre now, smuggled up from the Republic."

"How'd you meet Plastino?"

"Through friends," said Penny. "There's the hotel, with the cross on top."

"Oh, that's right. They turned the San Arturo Mission into a hotel a few years back," said Haley. "I don't visit this town much."

"Don't worry. You can bribe your way around here as easy as in San Rafael." Penny was tapping with her fingers again.

The New Punch And Judy Theater was whitewashed plaster, arches, red tile, colored glass. A banner announced *Last Time Tonight*. Haley slowed in passing. "Where does Plastino live?"

"Here. He's got a combination office and apartment in the little courtyard behind the theater. You use that alley right there. It's a small adobe house."

"Who were the people who introduced you to him?"

"Nobody to concern you. Some friends. I know people all over California. Just some friends," said Penny. "I had his name. See, I was here in San Arturo with somebody, Jim. No, he's not here now. We came here for a few weeks, stayed. A long time for me. Events got somehow dreadful and I was by myself. I had Buddy's name and I thought he might know of some kind of job around here, or at least might stake me. Instead he recruited me into the Lady Day movement." She exhaled sharply and turned to frown at the yellow adobe walls of the old real estate office they were now passing. "I'm cheerful these days compared to what I was like then, Jim. I guess Buddy hit me exactly when I was in the mood to get involved with that collection of nasty . . ."

"Nasty what?"

"Girls. Nasty broads," said Penny. "Mean bitches. I'm like that myself at times."

Haley headed the green car for the hotel. "These Lady Day girls, are they in town? Will they spot you?"

"No. Most of the groups drift. They camp someplace, move on. Then, when I was here a couple of months ago, this particular group was holed up, a half dozen of us, at an old ranch house about ten miles out in the country from here. Buddy took me out there the first time."

"Can we check there?"

"They moved on," said Penny. "Which is when I slipped away, got off that merry-go-round."

"Where did they move to? What was their next camp site going to be?"

"I don't know."

"How many of these Lady Day groups are there?"

"A few dozen probably."

"And why is Lady Day killing?"

"I don't know all the plans and workings," said Penny. "I was a novice, a neophyte. Nobody sat around and showed me maps and charts and scrapbooks full of snapshots of Lady Day at work and play, after all. Stop playing private inquiry with me for awhile, Jim."

"Okay."

Walking by the entrance to the ramp leading into the courtyard of the converted mission were two local cops, uniformed in earth colored tunics and riding breeches. "Some more people you can bribe," pointed out the girl.

Haley drove onto the red tile ramp. "I know," he said. "Our office isn't on very good terms with the San Arturo locals, as I recall. They don't much like the S.F. Enclave law either here. The locals are crooked in a particularly insulated way, and tough to reach."

"Smile at them."

The courtyard of the mission hotel was walled with thick adobe walls. From behind a fountain scurried a bellhop dressed as a vaquero. "I'm real," he announced, opening the door on Penny's side. He wore ornate vest and pants, silver trimmed boots.

"Real what?" Haley stepped out of the machine, stretched. Doves came swooping at the bright spray of the fountain.

"A real person. A living human being," the bellhop explained. He was pale and forty under his Mexican cowboy stain. He groped in the car, feeling for luggage. "Lots of the staff here is mechanical. Hardware, robots, androids. They even have a robot of Father Serra, founder of the mission, saying mass in the chapel. You have no baggage?"

"No."

The man took off his sombrero, rubbed at his thin sweated down hair. "Usually they're pretty liberal here, but our mayor has been on a civic decency binge lately. We have to be a little more cautious. So it'll cost you twenty bucks extra to register together and no questions asked. Give me thirty and I'll fix it up." He put his sombrero back on tight. "The reason I informed you I was human is so you could tip me accordingly. Guests tend to mix me up with the gadgets a lot and not tip. I've taken to speaking up."

Haley grinned and took out his wallet. "Twenty for the desk, five for you."

"I usually get ten."

"Five," Haley told him. "One of the disadvantages of not being a machine. People can bargain with you."

The bellboy said, "Very well, sir, five it is." He grabbed the cash, then called out, "Hey, Pedro. Park this car."

A big android in serape and white peon clothes shuffled over, bowed, and sat himself in the car. "*Suerte*," he said and drove off.

"He's wishing you good luck," said the bellhop. "I'll go in and settle matters with the desk. You and the young lady meet me in five minutes or so. *Adios*."

Penny had strolled to the fountain and was standing facing it, her hands locked behind her back. "We didn't have to bribe anyone the last time I stayed here," she said when Haley reached her.

"I bring out the monetary in people."

"Would you mind much if I walked around town for awhile, by myself?"

"Yes."

"It will be safe. The Lady Day bunch, they're long gone. Buddy usually sleeps most of the day."

"Possibly." Haley put a hand on her shoulder. "I think we should stay together for now. Tonight I'll check some things out. And you'll stay safe in the hotel."

"Protective custody."

Haley didn't respond.

When the bellhop waved to them from the lobby entrance, Penny took Haley's arm and smiled. They walked into the mission hotel together.

XII

THE TWILIGHT awoke him. Haley sat up, still naked, in the sleeping pit. He reached over to touch Penny, turning as he did. His knobby fingers touched nothing. Haley blinked the last of his drowsiness away, looked around the shadowy room. "Penny," he said. "Hey, Penny."

He swung up into the high cool silence of the room. His foot slid on a tri-op post card. Picking the card up, he noticed a message, half printing, half writing, from the girl. "Changed my mind again. Just like me, isn't it? Am out exploring the town. Will catch up with you after the show tonight. Someplace. Probably right here. Still fond of you. Love, Penny."

The mission bells rang for the hour of seven. Haley rubbed at his chest with one palm. "Damn." He picked up his underwear and another post card fell out. "Don't worry so much. Love again, Penny."

Haley crossed the thermal hemp rug and went into the shower unit. He forgot to set aside the two cards and the messages ran and dripped pale blue spots on his stomach and knees. A small speaker grid wedged above the shampoo spout crackled on and said, "The water you're enjoying comes from an artesian well sunk many long years ago by Father Marco Haifolli and blessed by him. The management and staff of the San Arturo Historical Mission Inn Hotel sincerely hope you are enjoying this shower."

"It's holy enough. But can you get it a little warmer?"

"Bottles of San Arturo Historical Mission Inn Hotel water are for sale in the Souvenir Sacristy on the ground floor," said the speaker grid and clicked off.

Haley left the stall, stepped into the hot air booth, left it half dry, put on the same clothes he'd had on before. He hurried out of the rooms and to the elevator.

The operator was an android, dressed as a Franciscan friar. "Bless you, sir. Main floor?"

"Yes," answered Haley. "Did you take a girl down, rangy brunette, high cheek bones?"

"Yes."

"When?"

"We like to respect each guest's privacy," said the brown robed android.

"We're together, she and I."

"Ah, yes. So. Imagine somebody shacking up here when this place was a mission, huh? Well, other times, other customs."

"I thought you were programmed to be humble and reverent?"

"Two years in this place would turn a saint into a rascal," the android said. "The things I see. Took my faith clean away. Your girl left a good hour or more ago."

"Alone?"

"Ah, yes. So. Jealous, I imagine? I don't blame you. Nice looking girl, though on the slim side."

"I meant she wasn't forced to go by anyone?"

"She was alone."

"Any idea where she was heading?"

"She mentioned she was in a wandering mood, nothing more, sir."

The car hit the first level, opened. Haley cut fast across the lobby, pushed the oaken doors hard, hit the street. Swallows were flickering down through the fading day, landing in the tree tops. Haley felt an odd tightness in his chest. He rubbed his palm against his ribs, turned to the left.

There was no sign of Penny in the art gallery next to the mission, no sign of her in the Gato Loco Restaurant, where a mechanical Mexican played a metal guitar. No sign of her in the Mission Greeting Gadget Shop, where two spare ladies from Oakland were buying a Get Well Clock for a dying uncle. Haley kept on looking.

When the curtain went up at the New Punch And Judy Theater, Haley still hadn't located Penny. He sat in his back of the theater aisle seat and kept studying the small crowd even as the lights faded down.

The woman next to him looked to be the one who'd bought the souvenir clock. She turned to him, smiled a frail smile, and said, "I'm going blind."

Haley said, "No, they only turned off the lights."

"Yes, I'm aware of that. I mean, medically speaking, I'm going blind."

"Do you want me to find you a doctor?"

"I'm not complaining. It's a slow thing. We all have our cross to bear. As it is, I'm better off than my uncle. He's up in Oakland dying this very minute," the spare woman said. "I was going to ask you to read my program to me. I'm on a vacation with another teacher from the Oakland Lift Up The Poor Trade School. She's slowly going deaf and didn't care to attend the play. I have no one to read for me."

"Shut the crap up," said a plump Negro man to the front of them.

A blonde teenaged girl next to him said, "Don't

use dirty language with a blind lady, you blacka-moor."

"You can shut the crap up, too, missy," replied the black man. "I came here to enjoy this anti-feminine play. I share an anti-feminine view with this troupe and you and the old bimbo with the big bazoo are adding to my bias right now."

"Well, I don't think you should say crap to a blind person."

"That's all right," called out the frail woman. "I'm only partially blind, young lady."

"In point of fact," said the fat black man, "I happen to be totally sightless myself. You may even have heard of me. I'm a blues singer, Blind Sunflower Slim."

The teenaged girl said, "Who cares? Blues are outmoded. Mechanical jazz is what's of the moment."

"Shut up," cried a redhaired Negro man from across the aisle.

"That's my partner," said Blind Sunflower Slim. "That's Cripple Memphis Red himself."

"None of you sound in very good shape," said the young blonde.

"At least I ain't up in Oakland dying," said Slim.

Haley cleared his throat and said to the woman next to him, "The program tells us the play we are about to see tonight is entitled *Hello, Bluebeard, Hello!* It's described as 'an anti-feminine tragi-com-edy & encounter' and it features Maxwell Arnold, Jr. as Bluebeard, C. Gillis Lumbard as Aunt Polly, D. W. Fulmer as the Current Mrs. Bluebeard and Mr. Plastino himself as Bluebeard's Mother."

"Hey," said Slim. "The curtain's been up five minutes and I ain't heard nothing but interruptions."

"Quiet, Slim," said Haley. "Or I'll tell the local cops not to let you work your dodge here."

Slim twisted around, frowning. "Oh, hello, Haley. How are things in Frisco?"

"About the same." To the woman Haley said, "This scene takes place in the castle of Bluebeard. Now let's all relax."

"Thank you, sir," said the woman.

On the stage a small young man in doublet and hose was waving a sword. "Honestly," he said, "this is the limit. I don't know why I keep getting married."

His wife, played by a plump forty-two year old man in a blonde wig, entered through an arched doorway of the simple castle set. "Now what, schmuck?"

"You know very well what. Don't now what schmuck me."

Mrs. Bluebeard put her palms against her bosom. "You're always accusing me of something. But I assure you I have been faithful."

"I don't care about that," said Bluebeard. "I just don't like you messing around with my stuff."

"Well, I can't help tidying up. A woman's work, you know."

"I've told you and I've told you not to fool with my closets. Now haven't I?"

"This castle is such a big place to keep clean by itself," replied his wife. "I should think you'd praise rather than criticize me."

"Didn't I hire you a serving wench and a maid of all work?"

"Yes, but then you turned around and murdered them," complained his wife. "And that maid was a real help."

"Well, I waited until her day off to murder her." Bluebeard stepped to the light strips which made up the footlights. "What would you folks do in a situation like this?"

A pale young man in the front row stood up and said, "Kill that bitch."

Mrs. Bluebeard stalked to the footlights. "Okay for you, Ralph. I see you. You're always the first one with that suggestion. Every night."

"You asked for an encounter." Ralph hopped upon his chair and peeled off his paisley print tunic, waved it in the air.

"Wait, wait now," said a gray man in the fifth row. "I used to be like you fellows. I had a lot of hostility in me. You know what caused it? Fear, simple fear."

"Oh, Christ," said Bluebeard. He leaped off the stage and trotted up the aisle.

"$4000 it cost me to learn this important lesson," said the gray man. "You fairies I'm telling it to for free. You wouldn't hate dames if you didn't fear them. See?"

Bluebeard clunked the man with his sword hilt.

"See that?" cried Mrs. Bluebeard from the stage. "That's how he treats me, too."

"This is nonsense," said a big dark man in the sixth row. "You folks all know me. I'm your town mayor, Mayor Herriman. Now, as you all know, I'm all for live theater, but I just feel I have to say something. Folks, there's no love here. Why, folks, the greatest thing in the world is love. Love between a good man and an honest woman. You know, folks, the only thing in the whole wide world better and truer is the love of a mother for her child."

"Did somebody call me?" Through a simulated oaken door on the stage stepped a tall handsome man dressed as Bluebeard's mother. It was apparently Buddy Plastino.

"Hiya, Buddy," shouted Ralph, who had all his clothes off now.

"Author, author," cried about a third of the audience.

Buddy kissed his fingers, bowed, laughed. He undid his gray wig and waved it in the air, revealing curly blond hair beneath. "Son," he said when the ovation had subsided, "come back here and give thy old mother a kiss on her fair old cheek."

Bluebeard dropped the unconscious gray man in the aisle and said, "Coming, mother."

Haley, bent low, left his seat and moved quickly through the darkness and out of the playhouse.

Haley went down the alley Penny had pointed out that afternoon and found himself in the small tiled patio she'd said would be behind the theater. No lights burned here and Buddy Plastino's low adobe cottage stood quiet and dark.

In under five minutes Haley located the alarm system and got it turned off. He picked next the locks on the succession of doors leading to Plastino's private office and then spent fifteen minutes thoroughly searching it. When he unscrewed the lip of the now turned off disposal hole, Haley found a half folded slip of paper clinging to the trap. The paper was of good quality, pale yellow. It had a medical RX on it, but no name. Scrawled in green ink was: *Tonight it is, as planned. Doc.*

Haley found nothing else suspicious in the small house, nothing that seemed to pertain to Lady Day or Plastino's involvement with her. Leaving the still adobe building exactly as he'd found it, Haley went back to the playhouse.

The theater lights were all on. Two of the actors were pulling the clothes off the blonde teenaged girl. Buddy Plastino was in the orchestra pit wrestling with Blind Sunflower Slim, who was trying to brain him with the spare woman's souvenir clock.

Sitting in the second row near the aisle, watching and looking worried, was Penny.

XIII

HALEY PUSHED forward, eyes fixed on Penny. A tweed elbow hit into his stomach, spinning him slightly. A shawl entangled itself with his left leg. A black bare arm rose up and his chin struck it. A dozen more people twisted and pushed into the aisle. Haley ducked low, dodging elbows, knees, fists. A fat freckled red-haired girl fell tree-like in his path, her hands folded over Bluebeard's sword.

· "Wench," shouted Bluebeard, whose beard had fallen off, "return my broadsword."

"Actually that's a rapier," corrected a Talmudic scholar who was helping lift Bluebeard into the air like a battering ram.

Haley sidestepped. He tripped over a bundle of rope-tied computer program cards, went to his knees. Two fourteen year old girls danced on his back.

"Give that here now," said Bluebeard's present wife. His wig was being thrown high by a motorcycle salesman.

"What are we learning from this encounter?" a fine boned Chinese girl asked her escort.

Haley erupted from the aisle floor and pushed on. Three rows ahead of him was the big dark Mayor Herriman. The mayor was frowning and a look of surprise was growing on his face, paling it.

Haley noticed what the mayor had noticed. "Damn."

Four girls were striding across the stage. From the rear entrance, walking straight and tall to the footlight strips. All in black. Black tights, black knee boots, black pullovers. Hair held back with black cords. Each carried a blaster, in casual ways. They moved together, side by side. They leaped the footlights.

"Penny," shouted Haley through cupped hands. "Penny, get out of here."

The Lady Day girls used their rifles as prods, clearing a path in the scrambling crowd. Penny was on her feet, but blocked by four tangled, fist fighting businessmen. Her face narrowed, the cheekbones undercut with deep sharp shadows. She tapped at her chin with a half formed fist. She didn't hear Haley, nor see him.

One of the black clad girls spotted her. A tall chunky girl, her hair a dizzy shade of orange. The plump girl stirred the crowd out of her way, knocked heads, booted groins. Penny jumped to the seat of her chair. The orange haired Lady Day girl sprang and caught Penny around the throat with the rifle barrel.

"Stop," roared Haley. He punched people, striving to reach Penny.

The other three black dressed girls had clutched the mayor. He seemed unconscious and they were backing for the stage with him.

"Dumb pecker head," yelled a fat boy Haley stepped into. He punched at Haley's flat stomach.

Haley thrust the boy aside and jumped.

The closest Lady Day girl, a lovely Negro girl, noticed him. Her nostrils flared. "Back off."

Haley kept coming.

The black girl gritted her teeth and her mouth went thin and gray. The rifle ripped up and the butt smacked straight into Haley's chin.

He swooped involuntarily. Cried out, tottered backward. Then slumped over an aisle seat arm. The crowd unwound around him, dimming and disconnecting. Sound and light grew fuzzy, intermittent. Everything vanished.

Haley had lost a piece of time. How much, large or small, he wasn't yet sure. A brown uniform was next to him. And only a few of the audience. Haley inhaled, choking, stood straight.

"Everybody step aside," said the San Arturo local cop. "Let us sift for clues."

Three other earth color uniformed locals were up on the stage. So was Buddy Plastino, wigless, sitting in an alcove beneath a stained glass window with the hair in his lap.

Penny was gone. So was Mayor Herriman.

"Out of the way, folks," repeated the local cop. "Line up in the lobby if you want a ticket refund."

Haley climbed onto the stage. He went to Plastino and grabbed the blond actor by his laced bodice. "Where'd they take her?"

Plastino smelled of lemon blossoms. "We've had enough roughhouse for tonight, haven't we? Take your hands from me, whoever you are."

"I'm Haley. Frisco PI. Where did your Lady Day girls take Penny Deacon?"

Plastino brought up the hand with the wig and shoved at Haley. "I only listen to gibberish and bad dialogue when I'm paid for it. Officer, remove this man. He's intimidating your key witness."

The youngest, tallest local cop ran over. "Back off, bud. What's going on?"

Haley let go of Plastino. He looked at the tall cop, whose hand rested on his hip holster. Haley knew the locals weren't cooperating with the Private Inquiry Office. He didn't know what their relationship with Plastino might be. He moved a few steps back. "I want a refund. I had an orchestra seat."

"Out to the lobby then, bud," the cop told him. "You come in the wrong direction."

Plastino watched Haley, patting at his damp chest with the maternal wig.

"Thanks, officer. My mistake." Haley left the stage by a side stairway. He pushed through the nearest exit door, ran down the alley he found himself in and to the rear of the playhouse.

The stage manager was a very old man with subdued makeup. He had a tan overcoat tossed over his shoulders and was standing at a rear exit, explaining things to two more local cops. "Honey," he said in his old throaty voice. "I saw those four bitches as close as I'm seeing you."

The cop with the moustache said, "Watch the language."

The stage manager sighed. "They went rampaging by me and they turned left at the mouth of the alley there. I was out signing programs for a few of my young admirers and the spade bitch knocked my jap lettering pen clean out of my hand."

Haley walked on by the group.

"Who are you?" called the moustached cop.

"Looking for the box office to get a refund."

"Up the alley and to your left, honey," the stage manager said.

"Thanks." Haley went on and was soon in shadow. At the end of the alley he went to the right. It figured the stage manager knew about the plan to grab the mayor. Meaning his eye witness account wasn't worth much.

Haley walked quickly on for a block. Then began asking questions. The man who ran the *Potato Heaven/101 Kinds Of Fries* sidewalk cafe had seen the retreating girls. "Four of them," said the man, who was sitting at one of his own tables and wearing a potato shaped hat. "Real lookers. Really, what we used to call when I was a young man, zoftig. That means amply built."

"Which way and in what?"

"Land car," said the potato man. "Couple years old, dark blue. Going like hell, but I had time to notice those girls. All dressed up in black and, like I say, zoftig."

"They went which way?"

"Down this way and then they shot left at the corner. That road leads by the old cemetery. It's one way you can pick up the old 101 highway. Want some fries?"

"No, thanks." Haley turned, ran back to where he'd parked his land car. He got in and drove the way the Lady Day girls must have gone.

Mist was dropping in on the night and the full moon was lost. Haley was passing the cemetery when its wrought iron gates swung open and a coffin on an electric cart came rolling out. The coffin came about twenty feet out of the gate and then turned around and rolled back inside the cemetery. A curly haired man with a low stomach had run the same

course as the coffin, following in its wake, waving a
brimless cap.

Haley swung in to the curb. He stopped his car
and got quietly out. At the now shut gates he called,
"Hey, in there."

"Don't go scaring him again." The man, wearing
the brimless cap now on his curly head, came on
tiptoe to the floral patterned grille work. "I only
just got him calmed down."

"I'm a Frisco Enclave private investigator," Haley
said. "Have you seen a land car going this way?
About ten minutes ago, four girls in it. Maybe a couple others."

"Sure we did," said the man. "That's exactly what
started him off. Gave him a fright."

"Which way did they go?"   .

"That car came by so darn fast it shattered the
silence. Also sideswiped my garden tool barrow. I
hadn't as yet brought the darn thing in. So all that
noise scared him and he's been either hiding among
the headstones or trying to run off since."

"Any idea the direction the car headed?"

"Sure, I can tell by the sound. It climbed at the
fork up there, meaning left and inland. That's the
uphill road, away from the Pacific. Used to call that
road the Camino Real, I think."

Rattling commenced behind him. "Spooks, spooks.
Let me out of here." The electric coffin wagon was
rushing at the gates again.

"There's absolutely nothing to get upset about,
you fool machine." The gravedigger put both of his
hands in a stop gesture.

"Spooks. Creepy stuff. Oh boy, let me out of here," said a small speaker grid in the base of the cart.

"He's on the fritz again," the gravedigger told Haley. "Talking crazy through his elegy box." The fore coffin handle hit him in the paunch and he fell aside.

Haley was back in his car by the time the cart came looping out of the cemetery, chased by the gravedigger.

Haley drove on, worried, following a vague trail. He was thinking of Penny.

XIV

HALEY LET the land car drive itself while he yawned, took his hands from the steering bar, stretched his arms up. His left shoulder made a splintering sound and his backbone ratcheted faintly. He puckered his mouth, blinked and gripped the steering bar again. It was cold early morning all around, mist rolling out of the low gray hills. Haley felt a momentary tightness across his chest. He had been driving and searching now since last night and no sign of Penny.

"Think about something else," he said aloud.

He pushed the car radio ON button and the radio said, "That's right. Still one big hour left on the All

Night Grievance Show. Sleepy Joe Bryan still right here with you. Okay, listener, you're on. What's your bitch?"

"Listen, you dumb bastard, this is the little old widow lady from Fresno. It seems to me you and most of your listening audience are cockeyed in your theories about these so-called Lady Day murders. Now as I see—"

Haley pushed OFF.

In a thin patch of fog parts of a cottage style motor lodge showed. Orange letters blinked the name *G-Man Motel* fuzzily. Haley left the highway and drove through the lathe arbor entranceway. He parked on damp gravel next to an apple tree. As he was sliding out of the car he frowned at the radio speaker.

"Maybe she's got a valid theory." He turned the show back on.

"They live in Mount Shasta and send out little messages through rocks," the widow was saying. "Next time you're around a boulder, listen, pay attention. For attention must be paid. They'll tell you about Lady Day."

"The talking rock theory," said Sleepy Joe Bryan. "We called Doc Robeson at Frisco Enclave University about three hours back—where were you then? Dozing?—and he assures us the talking rock theory is full of crap."

"Oh, bullshit it is," insisted the widow. "A rock could fall on your Doc Robeson and he wouldn't ..."

Haley left the car. Five strides across the gravel

a spotlight hit him and a voice called out, "Okay, mitts in the air. Freeze and no funny stuff."

"What branch of the law are you with?" Haley asked the wide old man who approached him, sub-machine gun aimed.

"No lip. Raise those hands. March on into the registration office. We got a vacancy."

"I expect you would," said Haley, crossing the gravel. "I want information, not a room."

"Button your lip and march." The old man wore a rumpled past-style dark suit. One that required a white shirt and a wide striped tie. "Everybody who visits the G-Man Motel gets the same treatment. We respect everyone's civil rights, regardless of race, creed, color or place of national origin. Speaking of which, you're a Romanian, aren't you?"

"No."

"We'll find out eventually. Of course, you're perfectly within your rights to clam up. We still follow the Constitution around here. That's the Constitution of the United States of America. I don't know if you've heard of that in Romania."

"Oh, yes, it's one of the reasons I came over." Haley opened a glass paned door.

The motel office was a big room with a linoleum rug on its floor. Six desks in two rows, an American flag on a standing staff next to a blue tinted water cooler.

On a wooden waiting bench a pretty blonde girl sat with her arms folded and her head cocked far to the right. At the nearest desk a freckled young man was being interviewed by a small old man in a flannel bathrobe.

"Sit down," ordered the man who'd brought Haley.

The old man at the desk had brown hair that stood straight up. His eyes and mouth were rimmed with wrinkles and his voice came from high in his nose. "Did you frisk him?"

"Darn it," said the wide old man with the machine gun. "No, sir. I'm sorry."

"Skip it. I'll handle the matter. Get back on outside, 23."

"I'm 27."

"Well, we're all getting older and more forgetful. Out."

The young man slowly moved, crouching, out of his chair. "We'll stay at another place. That'll be okay. Good night."

"Nonsense," said the wrinkle-rich old man. "The G-Man Motel is the finest in the area. Not only are our rooms spacious, they contain twenty-five servomechanisms for your comfort and pleasure. Besides, which, in each unit you'll find there are relics of famous crimes." He patted a card on his desk. "In your room, for instance, you'll find John Dillinger's death mask, Machine Gun Kelly's overcoat and a photomural of the last hours of Julius and Ethel Rosenberg."

"We only wanted a quick place to shack up," the blonde girl told Haley. "Bunny and I are having an affair, is what it is."

"How long have you been in this office?" asked Haley.

"Couple hours," said the girl. "The old guy is the former Director of the Federal Bureau of Investigation. His name is William Francis Jacovetti. Ever hear of him?"

"Yes, in school."

"I wish we had, Bunny and I. My husband'll be back at the auto camp in a couple more hours. The course of true love never goes too smooth, is what it is."

"Did you notice a group of girls, dressed in black, driving a dark blue late model land car, out on the road?"

The blonde shook her head. "When I'm with Bunny I notice very little. You're oblivious when you're really in love, is what it is."

Jacovetti said to Bunny, "Young man, all we need now is your footprints."

"I don't want to offend you, Mr. Jacovetti, really," said Bunny. "Except we're in sort of a hurry."

"Nonsense," said the former FBI man. "You'll never regret the thoroughness you meet here at the G-Man Motel. I run it exactly like the FBI."

Sighing, Bunny asked, "Which foot?"

"Both of them."

"That's a big ink pad you have."

"I can print two people at once if I need to."

"Boy," observed the blonde. "If my husband ever gets a private detective on to us, we're finished. I can just see that waspish lawyer of his holding up Bunny's bare footprints in a court room."

"We check all footprints out with Washington, D.C.," said Jacovetti.

"Washington, D.C.?" asked Bunny. "Isn't it still collapsed?"

"Some of the computers are still alive. We brought a lot of our own computer equipment out west when we moved. I have, I can assure you, access to millions of footprints."

Bunny looked at the sunlight starting to show faintly at the slat blinded windows. "Could I come back and finish this some other time, Mr. Jacovetti? I honestly have to get Dia Leah back to her vacation site soon."

"You're acting more and more like a fugitive from justice, young man."

"If I'm not back in the trailer in two hours we're all going to be fugitives," said the blonde Dia Leah.

"Mr. Jacovetti," said Haley, standing. "I'm here on Private Inquiry Office business. Can I interrupt?"

Jacovetti's wrinkles expanded from around his eyes and mouth. "PI? From Frisco?"

"Right," said Haley.

"Well, it's been some time since you boys called on the Bureau for cooperation." He handed Bunny a brass key. "Room 23. Go away."

"Thanks." The blonde stroked Haley once at the small of his back. "I hope you find your lost girls."

After Jacovetti shook hands with Haley he kept hold of him and rolled Haley's fingers over the giant ink pad. "I sincerely hope you don't mind my using footprint ink. It's just as good. Clean, too. We change it once a day. I insist on a thorough record of everyone who comes into my place."

"I'm looking for a party of four girls, all wearing black clothes, pants and pullovers. They have a fifth girl as a hostage, and the mayor of San Arturo." Haley didn't sit down. "They would probably avoid your particular motel."

"Sounds like the Lady Day mob," said the old FBI man.

"Yes. Have you seen or heard anything?"

"Sit down. I don't get much chance to talk shop with a fellow professional anymore."

Still upright, Haley said, "I want to keep moving."

"Nonsense, you look to have been at this most of the night. Take a break. Cup of coffee?"

"Okay." Haley allowed himself to relax into the chair.

Jacovetti poked a button on his desk top. "Sorry to say I haven't seen hide nor hair of your Lady Day girls. Sounds like they're going in for kidnapping."

"Yeah."

Agent 27 burst into the office. "Shall I drop him, sir?"

"Bring us two cups of coffee."

Haley asked, "You have computers here?"

"I got a bunch of them," said Jacovetti, his smile paralleled by wrinkles. "Go on, 27, get that coffee. On the double."

"Okay, sir."

Haley asked, "Are you hooked in with the S.F. Enclave Intelligence and Investigation Office Data Bank or the Sacramento Fact Pool?"

Jacovetti closed his eyes for a moment. "Well, yes, we are. Although I'm not sure if they're aware of it. We, with our usual FBI knowhow, tapped into their computer lines. Why?"

Haley drew out the prescription blank he'd found at Buddy Plastino's office. "I want to trace this. Paper, handwriting. Maybe I can do it here."

The old FBI chief said, "Sure thing. We have a big portable computer in a trailer out next to Cabin 26. She'll do the job. I drove all the way from Washington, D.C. with that baby. A few days after the United States wĕnt into its decline."

"Brought some of your agents with you?"

"Yes, six of my closest associates. We'd all of us nursed a dream of some day retiring to California. Those Washington, D.C. winters can be dreadful. One morning when there were an exceptional lot of riots in the capital I said to my closest friend in the FBI, 'Well, 22, let's get out while the getting's good. We'll drive to sunny California and open that motel we've always dreamed about.' 22, he's been dead and gone four years now. You wouldn't have found a more rugged and masculine man, yet he never married. He was a lifetime bachelor. As I am. We all of us were, who came out, except for 33. And he was most anxious to get out from under the thumb of his wife. So we loaded up six big trucks and trailers with personal belongings and FBI curiosities and equipment and we came westward. Like the pioneers of old, our rugged and masculine ancestors. We opened the G-Man Motel and have never regretted it. Everything around here is run like the Federal

Bureau of Investigation and, though we don't do a land office business, we manage to keep our heads above water. Naturally we're not naive enough to think you can run a successful motel without having customers who are up to some kind of sexual mischief. You'd be surprised how much of that there still is, even this late in the 20th Century. I had thought it was a fad of the 1970s, but no. I allow a certain amount of sexual fooling around. That last couple are an example. I deduce they're an adultery case. We allow it. As long as they don't use dangerous drugs or mechanisms and don't advocate treason or make mealy mouthed pleas for the underdog while they're registered here, they can do as they please in bed."

Haley and the old FBI man were outside now, walking through the brightening morning. The mobile computer was housed in a silver trailer.

Agent 27 came running up after them. "Where do you want the coffee, sir?"

"In the computer room," said Jacovetti. "Obviously." He climbed up the metal step ladder and worked on the locks of the flaked silver painted door. "I have a combination padlock on here, plus one set to open only for my fingerprints."

"We used to have another lock for his footprint but he can't bend that way anymore," said Agent 27.

"We're all getting along in years," admitted Jacovetti. He took Haley inside and introduced him to the computer.

XV

THE FAINTLY brown seagull flapped up off its perch on the head of the decorative drugstore android. It swerved, flying low toward Haley, then angled away into the fog.

"Oops," said Haley, automatically dodging the ocean bird.

"Do that again," requested the doctor shaped android. He had *Pure Food & Drug Plaza* lettered in light beads on his tunic chest.

"Oops."

"How long have you been doing that?"

"Only since the seagull flew off your head."

"Huh," said the android. "Sounds like whooping cough to me." He tapped his lower chest and then his temple. "We all of us have, up here in our brain region, a whoop center which controls whooping. Sounds to me, son, like you might have trouble in your whoop mechanism."

"Is Dr. Rebecca Stoner on duty now? I understand she owns and operates this drug store." The computer back at the G-Man Motel had traced the prescription blank and handwriting to this drug store in the beach town of San Bonito.

"You just take yourself on inside and tell them you're suffering with whooping cough, son, and they'll show you the wide range of quick acting and relatively harmless remedies always in stock here at the Pure Food & Drug Plaza, largest operation of its kind in San Bonito." He clicked off.

Haley walked ahead as a nearglass door opened in front of him. The drug store was high and square, made of panels of different colored and different shaped synthetic glass. The afternoon was as gray as the morning had been and the kaleidoscope effect was dulled. No one seemed to be inside the big store. He wandered among counters, suspended shelves. "Hello," he called out.

An old man in seafaring clothes appeared from around a wall of vitamin packs. "Do you know which is best?"

"No," said Haley. "Have you seen Dr. Stoner around anyplace?"

"I mean between this one and this one." The old man held up two clear tubes of spansules. "These red and white ones or these blue and gold."

"I'd take the blue and gold."

"You've had experience with this product?"

"No, but those are my school colors."

"Come now," said the white whiskered old sailor. "I'm due to ship out later in the day. We're going after mutant fish and I expect to hit many strange ports of call before my cruise is done." His voice lowered, grew more rapid. "I'm concerned, as no doubt you will be when you reach my years, with my vitality. With my vim and vigor, if you follow my drift.

I have quite a reputation for raising cain in the remaining hellholes of the Pacific. I need a product that will assure my prowess."

"Maybe you ought to think about retiring from the sea." Haley noticed a fat, pleasant looking middle-aged woman standing far across the store. She was wearing a white uniform.

The old seaman said, "It's a tossup. I can't decide whether to buy myself Wham Bam! Or O Buoy!"

"Try both." Haley hurried off toward the medical appearing fat woman. When he was near he asked, "Dr. Rebecca Stoner?"

The woman chuckled, blushed. "Bless me, no. I wouldn't be so high faluting as to claim to be Doc Stoner. No, I'm Nurse Thelma, and darned happy to be." She made a sweeping, two armed gesture. "None of this drug junk for me. Contentment is the word for Nurse Thelma."

"Is Doc Stoner here?"

"Oh, no, but I'm sure I can help you." She reached out and rumpled Haley's hair. "You're too big and strong to be sick."

"Doc Stoner and I have mutual friends. I'm anxious to have a talk with her."

The nurse reached into a low pocket of her uniform for a pair of square rimless glasses. "I have to wear these. My only flaw, I guess, is a slight touch of vanity." She adjusted the spectacles, studying Haley. "You're skinnier than I thought, but still a nicely setup chap." She poked him lightly in the ribs. "I tried contact lenses for a time. Trouble there was, being such a jolly old soul, I have too many friends.

Lots of big merry outgoing so-and-sos who were forever coming around and slapping me on the back.
Whap, whap. Kept knocking my contact lenses right
off my eyeballs. What mutual friends?"

Haley said, "Buddy Plastino."

Fat Nurse Thelma giggled. "Isn't he the one?
Some people call him a sissy. To me, though, a boy
who's polite and soft-spoken is a real prize. Oh, I
admit he's got that streak of anti-feminism, but I
think he's faking it. Anyhow, none of us is quite
perfect." She chuckled some more, took a set of brass
knuckles out of another low pocket, put them quickly
on and clipped Haley a smash on the chin.

He went backwards, nearly falling. He tripped on
a bin of animal shaped kid vitamins. "Relax now,"
said Haley, starting to get up.

Nurse Thelma hopped and drop kicked Haley's
chin with her metal toed white shoe. "You old
smoothy, you. I bet you're that snoop Buddy warned
us about. PI or Frisco cop." She charged in and
jabbed Haley twice more in the face, while fouling
him with her left knee. She gave him a chop across
the back of the neck and this propelled him into a
low hanging shelf of alkalizers.

Haley grabbed at the chain hanging shelf, trying
to use it as a trapeze. He went halfway through a
swing and the two chains unhooked from the glass
ceiling. He dropped hard on his tail bone, falling on
a table of decorator color syringes.

Nurse Thelma broadjumped clean over the table.
"We don't much care for sneaks and snoops," she
told the groggy Haley. "I'm going to lay you out,

cutey, and truss you up and use some of our under the counter truth pills on you." Clutching him in the armpits, she hopped again and cartwheeled him into the wall.

The impact knocked down an advertising clock that read *Time For Dick's Snuff*. "Oops," said Haley.

"Which of these do you recommend?" the old sailor asked Nurse Thelma. He'd worked his way over to her during the conflict.

Nurse Thelma jiggled her glasses back into place and smiled at the old man. "Well, I use Wham Bam! myself."

"Say, that's plenty good enough for me." He took a Frisco dollar from his coat and held the bill toward the nurse.

Haley coughed, chewed on air, shook his head. He jostled himself upright. He bent once, swaying with dizziness, and grabbed up the fallen advertising clock. He lumbered ahead and whapped the preoccupied Nurse Thelma over the head.

She dropped the paper dollar and the half wrapped bottle of Wham Bam! She slumped, fell. Rolled half over, sighing.

"You hadn't ought to cold cock a lady," said the old seafaring man.

Haley mumbled, "Love and war." He stretched up in a crunching way, grimacing, yawning. He'd had two hours sleep back at the motel. He took his pistol out and gestured. "Get some cord, rope, something. You know how to tie knots, I assume."

"Certainly," admitted the old sailor. "You're not trying to get me to engage in some kind of criminal activity or worse, are you? Maybe you got me wrong. The kind of cain I raise in the hellholes of the Pacific is all straight, conservative. No kinky stuff."

Haley said, "I'm with the Private Inquiry Office out of Frisco."

"Do all you PI ops go around decking middle aged ladies?"

Haley shook his head. "She's my first. Get some rope."

"I'm shipping out shortly, as I told you. I really ought to be home packing things in my sea chest."

"Rope first." Haley pointed the gun more directly at him.

The fat nurse rocked slightly in the store room hammock and said, "Buffalo Bill."

In the palm of his knobby hand Haley held two more of the pastel colored pills he'd located in a bottle under the change making servomechanism at the front of the store. The label read: *Trooz, the HARMless Truth Drug. Another fine product of the Tijuana Enclave Pharmaceutical Organization. Trooz is a highly effective truth drug, recommended for home use (except where prohibited by law). Two pills administered orally are usually all it takes to make anyone talk and tell all. For more persistent withholdings use four Trooz and, at your own discretion, a little physical force. Non-habit forming. Keep all medicines out of the reach of children.*

Haley made an impatient sound. "Now, Nurse Thelma. I asked you where Doc Stoner had gone."

The old sailor was still in the room, hesitant in the doorway. "She told you."

"Buffalo Bill is a place?"

"It's a ship. The S.S. *Buffalo Bill*. Docked down at Pier 3, right here in San Bonito. Got in early this morning."

"Ship," agreed Nurse Thelma, eyes closed.

"Why is Doc Stoner there?"

"Buddy is sick."

"Buddy Plastino?"

"Some hooligans on the San Arturo police force roughed the poor boy up last night," said Nurse Thelma.

Haley stood back from the hammock, brushing the price tag with his knee. "Pier 3, huh?"

"Right," said the old sailor. "It's a tub load of sissies. They come down here every once and awhile to shoot motion pictures at Fort Bonito and around. They're a bunch of sissies who make cowboy movies."

Haley let the remaining truth pills drop into his trousers pocket. He sprinted from the drug store.

XVI

HALEY DROVE a hundred yards beyond the naked man. He hit the brakes, pushed the reverse button and backed carefully to the field of high dry grass he'd just passed. The man was sitting on a rock and eating a nectarine. He was short, shaggy, gap toothed.

"Hey, La Penna," called Haley.

The bushy Private Inquiry Office operative waved and stood up. He made a stay-down motion at the grass behind him and then came jogging over to the white pole fence at the roadside. "I was just knocking off a little," he explained.

"You've got a girl with you?"

La Penna finished the nectarine and flung the pit. He scratched at his chest hair. "A real nitwit, with hot pants. Hot pants and a bias against air conditioning. Our room at the Ancient Mariner Inn, the air conditioning rattles. So she wants to do it outdoors. There I am in the sack with the old salami ready for action and she says how can you make love with all that dreadful noise? Me, I can abandon myself anyplace."

"You still working?"

"Yeah, on the same involuntary prostitution business," La Penna told him. "This nitwit girl is a new lead. I left San Anselmo the same day you almost got bounced out of the Nixon tower. Boy, you ought to see the knockers on this girl. A skinny broad but a real pair of scones."

"What do you know about the S.S. *Buffalo Bill?*"

"You're always all business," said La Penna. "You never like to take even five minutes to talk about tits. Now this nitwit girl, all she wants to talk about is great books. The hundred great books of all time. Nobody ever got a hard on from great books."

Haley said, "I'm still working on the Lady Day case. I found Penny Deacon, but now they've got her. Somebody who may have information about her is on that ship. It docked here in town this morning I hear."

"Okay," said La Penna. "As a matter of fact, I know a couple guys on the *Buffalo Bill*. Met them a few days back, up the coast. I'm not a double-gator. These guys are straight. They're just on board that fag ship writing the script for this new swish film. It's going to be a gay patriotic technicolor Western." He rubbed at his stomach, making a sandpaper sound. "I can get you on board. You're in a hurry?"

"Yeah."

"I figured. I was going to try for one more with the nitwit over there." He shrugged. "Just as well. She'd probably complain. We get out here in the fog where there's no rattling air conditioner and she starts worrying about the humidity. Now, Haley, I enjoy a good conversation. But humping is special. I wouldn't say exactly screwing is sacred, but I don't like a lot of extra talking. Noise, or music, doesn't distract me. Nor screaming and cries of joy and ecstasy. Talk, though. I may have an especially sensitive diddlywacker. A voice pitched a certain way affects it. It goes limp. Fwap like that. In India they can work that on snakes. Maybe on your pecker, too. With the caste system they still got over there, I'm not sure who can screw who. You take this nitwit . . ."

"You planning to go on to the ship with or without clothes?"

"Oh, yes, sorry. I'll get the nitwit back safe to the inn and join you, fully dressed and in my right mind, in five minutes right here. The Ancient Mariner is only over that hill. Does that hill remind you of a tit?"

"No."

"People perceive nature in different ways." La Penna jogged back to the rock.

The S.S. *Buffalo Bill* was a rebuilt ocean liner. It had recently been painted a hot pink and most of its crew was dressed in Indian fashion. Going up the gangplank, La Penna said, "My cover story with these guys is I'm in the pill business. Outlaw stuff from Tijuana and the Canal Zone Enclave. They don't know I'm PI."

"Plastino will recognize me," said Haley. "So I want to avoid him. You'll have to search the ship for this Doc Stoner lady and stash her someplace where we can talk to her."

"She's over fifty, huh?"

"According to the retired FBI computer I talked to."

"And probably a dyke?"

"Probably."

"Of course, the FBI used to think everybody was gay," said La Penna, stepping onto the deck. "Still, even if she's straight, I'm not much for banging older stuff. An ancient broad can sense my heart isn't in it."

"Whoa," ordered a small old man in feathers and furs. He was placed just to the left of the gangway, in a folding canvas chair.

"La Penna," said La Penna. "The pill freak. Remember?"

The old man, whose small round head was topped with a chief's feathered headdress, answered, "The horny fellow with the moustache. I recall you. You gave me those Mex pills to help my brain."

"Right, Deadwood. And this is my associate. I'm making a new delivery to the writers." La Penna tapped the old man's buffalo robe. "This is Deadwood Anderson."

"The famous cowboy star," added the old man. "At the moment I'm doubling as studio guard. Remember me in the TV films of the 1960s?"

"No," said Haley.

"Had a horse called Streak. I was the last of the big nighttime TV stars with an identifiable horse," said Deadwood. "The latter-day cowboys can't ride much. I had Streak embalmed and I donated him to a college museum with an interest in popular culture. Partly as a sentimental gesture and partly as a tax writeoff. You ever see an embalmed horse? Quite something."

"Where are the guys scripting today?" La Penna asked.

"Down in Hold #2, which they've got turned into a saloon set," said the old cowboy. "Last minute changes in the script. In a way I'm happy Streak died. He wouldn't have taken to my dressing up like a redskin and working for a boat full of pansies."

La Penna tapped the old man on the shoulder and led Haley along the deck, through wooden doors and down a metal ladder. "He used to be gay himself, but he doesn't remember it anymore."

The #2 hold was now a replica of a Western saloon of the late 19th Century. Wooden tables, long wood bar, gilt framed mirrors, brass cuspidors. Four men were in the big room, around one table. The table held schooners of beer, recording equipment, an automatic typewriter.

"Good afternoon, fellows," said La Penna when the saloon doors had stopped swinging. "This is my associate. And these guys are George Owen Baxter, Alden Orczy, Rowland Firemont and John Drew Burden. Some of the best Western writers in the business."

"What did you bring?" asked Orczy, a small thin young man in a plaid cap.

La Penna took a pillbox from his trouser pocket. "These'll raise your IQ by 10 points. Just in from Mexico."

Orczy removed his cap and smoothed his straight hair. "That's what you told me about those last ones, La Penna. And they turned out to be Mexican jumping beans. I was sitting in my dumb cabin the other night, nervous, overwrought. I wanted to calm down and then your pills started jumping around. It's unsettling, like having dimly realized hairy spiders skittering inside your skull."

"I didn't say they'd help you relax. Only improve your IQ."

"Horse cock," said the fat bearded Rowland Pine-mont.

George Owen Baxter, a tall, high foreheaded man in a scarlet jumpsuit and yellow shoes, said, "Rowland wants to get back to the script, Alden. You'll have to settle your addictions later." He looked up at Haley. "This is Rowland Pinemont. He's tops."

"Horse cock," said Pinemont.

"Dialogue isn't his forte," explained Baxter. "It's plots. He's a fount of plots."

"You guys," said Alden Orczy, strangling his plaid cap in his lap, "are just exactly mean like my first three wives. Bimbo #1, Bimbo #2 and Bimbo #3, as I call them. You have no concern for the heartfelt pleas of humanity, the nameless something that cries love in the harsh face of infinity."

"Horse cock," said Pinemont.

"Rowland is anxious to smooth out the rough spots in this film," said Baxter. "You can't expect the best plot doctor left in the world to share your petty concerns, Alden."

"You, you're like Bimbo #2," said Orczy. "No care for the unfortunate. Inside me is a soul which pleads, 'I have no shoes, but I must dance.' You schmucks strew broken glass in the footpath of my psyche."

"High noon," said Pinemont.

Baxter snatched up the automatic typewriter and plumped it into Pinemont's broad lap, slapping the mike into the big writer's fat hands.

"The sun is pasted to the burning sky like a scarlet cookie," dictated the bearded man. "A scarlet sugar cookie. Buzzards circle far off. We slowly, ever so slowly, truck across the heat crazed sands of Old California. The birds swoop and we, with stunning impact, zoom in. Zoom with dazzling speed and lock in on a tight shot of . . . of . . . horse cock."

"Don Diego," supplied Baxter. "The hero's name is Don Diego."

"Don Diego. His hand reaches up and slowly, ever so slowly, he peels the scarlet mask from his grim face. The mask is limp, like a scarlet pancake. He puts the mask in his saddle bag and from it, from the intricately carved leather saddle bag, he withdraws the deed to the hacienda." Pinemont lifted the typing machine off himself and reached for a beer.

John Drew Burden, the fourth writer, was small and thin. "Oh, that's really wonderful, Rowland. That's really brilliant. No wonder I'm only writing on this faggot movie until I get enough money to start a better society in the San Joaquin Valley. How'd the dumb deed get in his saddle bags?"

Baxter said, "Rowland gives us the bones, we have to flesh them."

Burden took off his plaid cap, which was similar to Orczy's. "This kind of film can't be done. A gay Western, yes. A patriotic Western, perhaps. A gay conservative Western, nix."

"The faggots didn't have enough money," said Baxter. "So they had to get outside financing, from wealthy citizens and from some groups like that Natty Bumpo Brigade up in Frisco. We don't have to waste time going over all that again."

"The title," continued Burden, "is maybe fair. *The Rio Rita Kid*. That's fair. The concept is not too awful. A sort of Robin Hood of the Old West. By night the mysterious masked avenger, fearless swordsman and peerless horseman. By day, the sweet new school marm. Good. I buy that. A nice switch on the old dual identity gimmick and it satisfies our faggot public. Myself I can't quite identify with a hero who goes around in drag. Still, I don't have to like the crap I write. What I can't cope with is how we rationalize his being against sex education in the schools."

"Well, he's the school marm," said Baxter.

"All the teachers I know are liberals."

"Yes, but how many do you know who go around in drag with a parasol and a blonde wig?" Baxter paused to sip his beer. "I see no big reason we can't integrate all the messages and still have a damn good action film."

Orczy's head snapped and he frowned at Haley. "What was that?"

"What?"

"Something rattling in your pocket." Orczy scowled at La Penna. "What kind of pills is your buddy carrying? What are you guys holding back?"

"We have other customers," said La Penna, squinting an eye at Haley.

Haley took the two loose truth pills from his pocket. "These are . . . well, they haven't run enough tests on them yet."

"IQ, calming, sex thrill or what?" Orczy caught hold of Haley's bony wrist.

"Beyond any of that. These are more mystical in nature.

Orczy picked the Trooz from Haley's hand and sniffed them. "They look familiar. They don't smell dangerous." He dropped the two of them in his schooner of beer and sloshed the contents around. "I'm a pill freak who doesn't like swallowing pills."

"Horse cock," said Pinemont.

"Rowland is very eager to get this scene done," said Baxter. "Shooting on this set is going to begin any moment now. When Rowland is creatively hot he likes to keep at it, press right along."

The saloon doors swung again and heavy boots hit the deck. Haley turned and saw a tall hefty woman in a cowgirl suit striding toward them. She was swinging a black medical bag in her right fist. "This must be Doc Stoner," Haley said to La Penna.

"You bozos will have to write Buddy out of today's filming," said the thick woman. "He's got to have nothing but rest and quiet for the next twenty-four hours."

"Horse cock," said Pinemont.

"Don't horse cock me, you bearded satyr." Doc Stoner flexed her broad shoulders and the fringe on her bolero danced.

"Rowland means," explained Baxter, "he's not sure who Buddy is, Dr. Stoner."

"He can't tell one fruit from the other," said Orczy.

"Buddy Plastino," said the doctor. "He arrived today to play the part of the Governor General of Old California, you little twit." She slammed her medical bag on the saloon table and snatched up Orczy's beer. "I see I have to help myself around here, since none of you straights will offer a lady a drink."

"We weren't sure you were a lady," said Baxter. "We thought you might be a guy."

Doc Stoner finished the Trooz laced beer, wiped her mouth on her wrist fringe. "Buddy Plastino may be a little too gay for your tastes and he may appear in fag Westerns too often in the role of Esperanza the Spanish Flamenco Beauty, but he is always a gentleman." Her voice had a burred growl in it. "He is always ready and willing to help a lady onto her horse and offer a drink when the situation seems to call for it." She took up Pinemont's beer next and quaffed it all.

"Horse cock," said the bearded author.

"Doctor Stoner," said Haley, taking the woman's arm. "Let us stand you to the next drink." He nodded at La Penna and the PI agent crossed to the saloon's bar and ducked behind it. Haley guided the doctor and placed her in a leaning position at the polished wood bar. "Two beers here."

"I'm a little woozy." Doc Stoner tugged at the brim of her sombrero and yanked it off. She fell sideways and banged against the bar. "This is interesting."

"You didn't unfasten your hat. It's still tied under your chin." Haley helped her to right herself, get the black hat off her short cropped hair.

"I am developing the classic symptoms of vertigo," said Doc Stoner. "I have the sensation I am whirling around and that the environment is also turning. The sense of balance, to be perfectly frank with you, comes partly from the sense of touch, partly from the sense of sight and partly from the mechanisms of the semicircular canals of the ear."

"What you're experiencing," Haley told her quietly, "is the side effects of the truth drug put in your beer."

"Of course," replied the doctor. "I should have realized. Actually, to be quite honest, I'm not actually a real doctor. I am actually a registered nurse and nothing more. My medical diploma is forged. It was forged by a little twit named Bernard Gruber of 1984 Laurel Street in Frisco. If the truth were known."

"What I'd like you to tell me now is the whereabouts of Penny Deacon," said Haley.

"I shouldn't tell," said Doc Stoner. "What did you put in that beer?"

"Trooz."

"I'm going to have to reorder that stuff. It really works. Although I may not remember any of this conversation. That's the way with a lot of these truth things, frankly."

"Penny Deacon," repeated Haley.

"If you must know, she's down in the Carmel Valley. At least, that's what Buddy says."

"Where exactly?"

"That funny farm place. That phony straight place that Dr. Hocktigon runs."

Haley recognized the name. "You mean the Vienna West Therapy Center?"

"That's the place. Old Hocktigon is in with the movement. The Deacon bitch is being held there for questioning. She tried to sell out the movement. Maybe to you. I don't know."

"Who's behind the movement? Who's Lady Day?"

"A mean bitch."

"Who is she? And where?"

"Get that old bull dyke off the set," called someone. "Out, out. All of you. We're rolling the saloon sequence of *The Rio Rita Kid* right now this minute." A slim brunette young man in a buckskin suit had entered. "You'll all be pleased to hear Buddy Plastino has risen off of what was practically his death bed to do a cameo bit as Esperanza the Spanish Flamenco Beauty."

"He's supposed to be quiet for twenty-four hours," said Doc Stoner. "Stomping his heels is not good for him."

"You feel like a saloon brawl?" Haley asked La Penna.

"Not much. Why?"

"Because Plastino just walked in with five wranglers and he's pointing at me. Let's leave Doc Stoner and find the back way out."

"Shouldn't we haul the old broad along for more questioning?"

"I want to find Penny, fast."

"Okay," said La Penna. "I know this ship a little. Come on this way."

Haley bolted over the bar as Buddy Plastino, lace shawl flowing and flapping, brought the band of heavies stalking toward the bar. Haley and La Penna stayed ducked until they were in back of the saloon set.

"Fire door," said La Penna, pointing.

Gun shots sounded in the saloon.

"Blanks," said La Penna.

Haley followed him through the metal doorway.

XVII

WHEN THE WHITE stallion heard the waltz music it snorted, reared up and did a little dance in the dusty roadway. Its plume fluttered and its white tail flickered and the uniformed rider slid out of the gilded saddle, tumbled leftward and thumped onto the ground. Haley swung his rented land car hard to left and missed hitting both the dancing horse and the fallen rider. When the thin man in the black and gold uniform sat up, Haley asked, "This is the way to Vienna West, isn't it?"

"Why the heck else would I be out here on this dumb Lipizzaner stallion?" The man dusted his puttees with buff gloved hands.

"Therapy?"

"No, I'm not goofy. I'm the gate keeper."

The road wound gently down through grassy fields and twisted cypresses. Haley nodded at the brightness all around. "I didn't notice the gate."

"Of course you don't. Because this smart alec

horse was running away with me." He jabbed a gloved thumb in the direction Haley was aimed. "The gate is one mile up that way. Right across the Blue Danube."

The white stallion snorted again and danced over to the man on its hind legs. The loudspeaker hanging in a nearby oak was not playing now.

"I meant Blue Danube River, dumbo, not Blue Danube Waltz," the gate keep said to his horse. "He loves to dance. They taught him at school. It's a liberal arts horse training school Dr. Hocktigon maintains here." He made a sudden swing at the animal with his riding crop. "Sit this one out, Rudy." To Haley the man said, "His name is Rudolf. Running away with me and dancing, those are his two main joys. That and those little crab apples that grow up in the hills. When he's really happy, he pisses. It's worse than the dancing. You a customer?"

Haley drew out a letter that La Penna had forged for him before going back to his own assignment. "My physician, Dr. Roger H. L. Winslow, suggested a few quiet days here. Here's a letter of introduction to Dr. Hocktigon."

The gate man waved the letter aside. "Save it. Just pay me the ten buck admission. Take your letter up to the T-Center. That's the pink building near the volksgarten."

Rudolf stopped dancing and began watching Haley. When he took a ten dollar bill from his wallet, the stallion licked his hand.

"He thinks you might also have little crab apples in there. Back off, Rudy."

Rudolf snorted and sniffed at the wallet, then clattered back. The loudspeaker began playing a new Strauss waltz. The stallion flicked his tail and galloped off into the nearest field.

"Will I be able to arrange an interview with Dr. Hocktigon himself?"

The black uniformed man was making a puckered face at the runaway horse. "He thinks that's cute now, playing games. Even after a liberal arts education horses remain basically dumb. Hey, stupid. No oats tonight if you don't come back in five minutes." He peeled back the lip of his glove and tapped at the square face of his wrist watch. "Beg pardon? You asked something?"

"My physician thought I ought to see Dr. Hocktigon himself. He went so far as to say it might do me a world of good."

"Hocktigon believes the total experience of Vienna West helps you when you're goofy. The gestalt of it, as he puts it." He turned, hands on hips. "Look at that dope out there. He thinks that's droll, doing the tango. Stop that dancing, Rudy. You've got three minutes left. Though if you want to pay $100 the doctor might grant you a ten minute interlude. You can check at the T-Center, the pink building facing Freud-Platz."

"Thanks. Want a lift back to the gate?"

"I can't return without Rudy. You go ahead. Have a good time."

Haley returned to his car and drove on through the valley.

Vienna West was compact and compressed, covering about a square mile and backed by an artificial forest. A small bridge of intricate wrought iron arched over the narrow artificial river. All vehicles were left on the Danube edge in a weedy parking platz.

Haley parked, then crossed the bridge. He grinned at the uniformed young man who was coming out of a candy striped guard house. "I ran into the gate keeper and Rudy out on the road and paid my ten dollars," Haley said.

"Oh, okay."

"Which way to the T-Center?"

"Beg pardon?" The young man had gray freckles and wore a visored cap three sizes too large.

"The Therapy Center, which direction?"

"Oh, yes, sure. Wait a sec and I'll look in the guide book for you. Or do you want to buy a guide book as a souvenir? No." He jumped back into the little guard house, came out with a red and white covered pamphlet. "I only started working here yesterday. What was that building?"

"Therapy Center."

"Oh, yes, sure. Let's see now." From directly over his head a loudspeaker on a pole was broadcasting string quartet music. "Let's see. Musikverein, Konzerhaus, Bohmische Hofkanzlei, Freud-Platz. Here. This must be it. With the big T drawn on it."

"Yes," agreed Haley.

"Okay, sure. Then you want to go right up this way. Across this platz and then take—see how my finger is going?—take Kolschitzky-Gasse, the street with all the coffee houses, and turn right at the first beer garden. Got that?"

"Thanks, yes."

"You don't look very screwy," said the young man. "Are you? I only began working here yesterday. I can't tell a screwball from a regular person. Which are you, if I may ask?"

"I'm goofy."

The boy sighed sympathetically. "That sounds serious."

"It's latent so far."

"Well, Dr. Hocktigon will fix you up. I hear all kinds of people come into VW screwy and go out pretty much normal. Of course, it's expensive."

"When you're goofy you don't care about costs. It's the cure that counts."

"Sure, you're perfectly right. That's really a healthy attitude to have. You sound better already and you're barely across the bridge." He frowned up at the loudspeaker. "What's going to drive *me* nuts is that old world music all the time. Me, I'm a mechanical jazz enthusiast. I suppose you, being along in years, comparatively speaking, go more for swing music."

"It depends on my mental state." Haley walked on.

Kolschitzky-Gasse was a crooked lane rich with weathered cafes and coffee houses, grillework, sea green tiles, polished wood doors, hanging metal lanterns, statuary, a coin operated fountain. Across the street from him, walking faster than any of the dozen visitors, Haley noticed a tall chunky girl. She had orange hair and a white nurse's uniform. Haley recognized her. She was one of the four Lady Day girls who'd grabbed Penny and the mayor. The girl entered a coffee house named Frau Goedewaagen's. Haley followed.

A rattletrap old android was playing the zither up on a carved wood platform near the entranceway. The room was low and round ceilinged. Its walls were carved wood panels spotted with tinted mirrors and glass ball lamps. Ten tables filled the small place, all but three unoccupied. The orange haired girl was not there.

"Ach zo," said the zither playing robot. "How vas you? Dot's good. Sid down. Haff zum coffee. Yah?"

At the nearest table sat a curly haired blond man and a pale skinned girl with blue-black hair. The man called to Haley, "He's on the blink a little. Pay no attention. His accent is dreadful, isn't it?"

"Shud up or giffs murder." The android was small and dented. His old blue suit was mended at all its bends. His metal arms and hands had been soldered and welded many times. A rusty bolt was loose in his plucking hand. "Vot a dodrotted platz dis is. Yah? Such a bunch uff vise guys. All screwy in der head."

"All part of the therapy," explained the blond man. "Don't allow him to rile you or make you writhe with anger. Don't let his nastiness unseat your reason and send sharp daggers of harsh pain through your vitals." He clenched his fists, bit his lip, then chuckled. "Join us, won't you?"

"King," said the pale girl, "maybe he doesn't want to relate to anyone. Perhaps he wants to sit in a dark corner and brood. Leave the poor man be."

Haley went to their table and took the remaining chair. "I will join you for a moment."

"See, Mary Alice. Be friendly and it produces friendship. Hi, my name is King Solomon McCurdy."

"Haley," said Haley.

"Haley, good. This is Mary Alice Cullen-Murphy. Our names sound a little alike, Mary Alice's and mine, but we aren't married. We aren't officially married. Simply living together."

"I'm his trial wife," said the pale Mary Alice. "His eighty-seventh trial wife."

"My problem, that's my problem," said McCurdy.

Haley nodded, then asked, "Did you folks notice a red haired girl?"

"Nurse Newberry," said Mary Alice. "She picks up three coffees to go every morning here. Back in the kitchen. She's employed up at the chateau."

"Chateau?"

"It's up in the Vienna Woods. Dr. Hocktigon lives there."

"My mother," put in McCurdy, "named me King Solomon because to her way of thinking the name connoted wisdom. To my regret, as I matured . . ."

"Grew up," said Mary Alice. "You haven't matured yet."

"Right. You're right to catch that, Mary Alice dear. As I grew up I suffered the wretched experiences of any child born late into a loveless, though fundamentally stable, marriage. I found King Solo-

130

mon was also famed for the number of wives he had. Perhaps you haven't noticed, Haley, but . . ."

"Of course he's noticed," said Mary Alice. "Everybody does."

"Right. Right you are, Mary Alice dear. Certainly, Haley you've noticed that one's name affects one's destiny."

"I have indeed," replied Haley. "Where exactly is the chateau, Miss Cullen-Murphy?"

"You can't miss it. The place is right near the Wilderness Encounter Camp Site. The chateau is quite large, mildly Gothic and richly encrusted with gargoyles and phallic symbols."

McCurdy went on, "My unfortunate first names explain why I've never . . ."

"Not never, King. You were three times."

"Right. Right you are, Mary Alice dear. My unfortunate first names explain why I've never been able to marry often. So now I soak up all the therapy I can get and hope for the best. Vienna West is swell."

Mary Alice said, "We really don't believe psychiatry has any validity in the modern world, but the atmosphere here, the . . ."

"Ambiance," said McCurdy. "The ambiance is swell, so pleasant. And the weather is almost always fair except for low morning overcast and fog along the coast."

"We enjoy the music, too," said the pale woman.

McCurdy cupped a hand to his ear. "Listen now, for instance."

From a distance of about a block away drifted the sound of boys singing. "King is fond of pseudo-religiosity," said Mary Alice. "Another problem of having a biblical name."

"It's actually a historical name."

The nurse with orange hair stepped from the kitchen with a plyosack of pastries in one chunky hand, a stack of three china coffee cups in the other. "Excuse me," Haley said to his host. "I'll skip the coffee and see a little more of the town. Thank you for your hospitality."

The boy's voices were marching nearer. "It's the Vienna Boys' Choir again," observed pale Mary Alice. "An android version."

"You have to look at these occurrences as challenges," cautioned McCurdy. "Tests. How one reacts is vitally important. That's a good part of what total environmental therapy is about. If you have the impulse to rend the little mechanical bastards asunder and scatter their wretched cogs and wheels and infernal mechanisms to the four winds, you mustn't." He chuckled. "A valuable lesson to learn."

"Your real problem isn't wanting to dismantle the robot Vienna Boys' Choir, King."

Nurse Newberry popped out of the door as Haley stood. He took three long strides and the wooden door snapped open again. In marched sweetly singing choir boys. All bright and fresh in old-fashioned bibbed sailor suits and straw hats. They sang, "Oh, tannenbaum, oh, tannenbaum," as they filled the little coffee house. Eventually two dozen of them were marching around in the low room.

"It's not Christmas, you dumb little gadgets," shouted McCurdy. He snarled and grabbed the closest choir boy, swooping the lad's straw hat from his head and sailing it in the direction of the zither player. "I think it'll be very good for me to smash a few of these urchins. Yes, very good."

"Let go, schmuck," said the choir boy.

McCurdy stooped, shook the boy. "A ringer? You're no android."

"I'm Dr. Hocktigon's prize nephew, schlep, and you better not frick around."

McCurdy gave the boy one more shake, reflectively. "Nephew, is it?"

"These andies keep breaking down. Today they were one short so I'm filling in. I have a very good voice, and a good ear."

"Oh, tannenbaum, oh, tannenbaum," sang the other twenty-three choir boys.

"They think it's the Christmas season," said the nephew. "They're always going blooey. They came in here for a hot toddy and a yule log."

Haley worked his way through the sailor suited boys. The orange haired girl was long gone now.

He saw no sign of her in the street. He stroked the knuckles of one bony hand, grinned a thin grin. He headed for the Vienna Woods.

XVIII

CROSSING THE simulated vineyard which bordered the forest Haley met a man wearing aggressive outdoor clothes.

"What time is it anyway?" asked the man. He was tall and taut, dressed in khaki. Spiked boots, a jungle hat. An antique .45 revolver was holstered on his right hip, a silver plated blaster on his right. A stun rod and a hunting rifle were slung at his back. Bandoliers and cartridge belts festooned him.

"Around eleven," Haley said.

The man plucked a purple grape from above, bit at it. "Synthetic rubber." He let the false grape fall and studied his wrist. "Eleven oh seven. Watch her bitch and moan when I get there."

"Who?"

"My wife. Everything is by the clock with her. I mean everything. I have to make love to her with an hourglass at the bedside. I'm Raleigh Swineherder and I lead these Wilderness Encounter groups. We got one scheduled to start at eleven sharp." He plucked another grape. "When we were first married it was a real *hourglass*. Then she took, in about our third year, to using one with only fifteen minutes worth of sand."

"You going to your camp site now?"

"I guess I better," said Swineherder. "Or Gloria will bitch and moan. You got yourself signed up with our Encounter gang?"

"No, I'm just strolling."

"You can't just stroll in the Vienna Woods," Swineherder said. "Unless you're a customer of ours. Or one of Hocktigon's special chateau patients."

Haley said, "In that case I'll sign on for your safari. How much?"

"Don't pay me. Gloria does all the bookkeeping. We charge a hundred bucks." Swineherder bit at another grape. "Synthetic rubber. They all are." This one he kept in his mouth, chewing at it. He made a wide come-on gesture and went tromping toward the woods.

"How many patients does Dr. Hocktigon have at the chateau?"

"Search me. He's a secretive little boob. Gloria gets along with him. I don't. Gloria is very outgoing. She's always taking him vegetable surprises." He selected a machete from the three dangling from one of his belts and began to hack at the thickening brush.

"Isn't there a path to your camp?"

"Sure, but this is better for you. Builds up the illusion you're in a real wilderness," explained Swineherder while chopping. "Gloria is always thinking up new ways to fix food. That little boob, Hocktigon, goes along with her. You should have seen his little boob face light up when she took him over a dish of her avocado surprise. You know what an avocado is?"

"Yes."

"Well, the part where the seed was, Gloria stuffed with elbow macaroni in wine sauce and rigged it to pop out when you open the avocado. So there's Hocktigon opening up his avocado and whap, a clump of elbow macaroni in wine sauce pops out and lands smack in his dish. The little boob nearly danced a jig." Swineherder's machete got entangled in some vinyl ferns and he halted to free the blade. "I try to eat out every chance I get. If you go along with this boob-oriented stuff of Hocktigon's I'm re-belling against Gloria in a symbolic way. On the contrary, the truth of the matter is I'm no boob. I say there are only so many ways you can surprise a man with vegetables and after that he's going to holler quits." They continued moving through the Vienna Woods.

"What size staff does the doctor have at the chateau?" Haley asked.

"Hard to tell," answered Swineherder. "He's got a mix of people and androids and servomechs work-ing there. Also the little boob is an attractive son of a gun. There's usually a few lady friends of his hanging around, helping out. I don't know, you might find thirty or forty in the place on any given day, people and andies."

"Not counting guards?"

"No guards," said the wilderness therapist. "No guards as such. There's a couple acres of ground surrounding the little boob's castle and it's all full of mechanical traps and electrified fencing. He's got, also, a pack of robot dogs. Big black devils, programmed to take a good healthy nip at anybody unauthorized. It's no place to go for a stroll. I have a hunch the little boob is over-protecting himself, but that's his problem. I've learned a few things on these Wilderness Encounters myself. Don't try to change other people. Learn to get along with their problems. Otherwise little boobs like Hocktigon will get under your skin. So will bitch and moan wives with hourglasses on the nightstand."

The artificial trees thinned and there was a circular glade. Bright in the midday sun, its grass intensely green. Four pastel colored real canvas tents were close together in the center of the clearing. A half dozen redwood picnic tables ringed its edge. At one of the tables stood a tall, not quite pretty, woman in an outfit similar to Raleigh Swineherder's. She was waving one hand at a large wicker basket on the table, while two women and three men looked from her to the basket.

"That's Gloria," said Swineherder, sheathing his machete.

Mrs. Swineherder was saying, "This is to be a voyage of discovery, this is. Twenty-four hours spent encountering ourselves and others. We are to experience the rigors of life in the wilds, we are."

"I still don't see why no dessert in our picnic lunch," said the chubbiest of the three middle aged men.

"This isn't a picnic," Gloria Swineherder told him. "This is a trek. A trek into the wilderness of place and the wilderness of self." She smiled suddenly at the man. "Don't fret, Mr. Grubert, you'll have all kinds of fun."

"But no dessert?"

"Shut up, Herschel," said the thin woman nearest him. "We're on this trek so you can shed some of your obsessions. One of which, believe you me, Mrs. Swineherder, is a real sweet tooth."

"Down there," said Grubert, pointing in the direction of the now not visible Vienna West, "you got pastry shops and coffee houses where I could eat strudel till it came out my ears. I was never happier. Yum yum."

"You don't believe me when I tell you this, Mrs. Swineherder, you don't know when you're happy and when you aren't, Herschel."

"What's wrong with I like to sit in a warm room and eat strudel and sip a little cup of coffee with cream in it?"

Smiling at her approaching husband, Mrs. Swineherder asked Grubert, "Suppose you tell us why that is so pleasant?"

"Why wouldn't it be pleasant? You eat strudel. It's got apples in it, nuts on top all chopped fine, a delicate sugary frosting, with cinammon sometimes. Anybody didn't like that would be a goon."

"He's always telling me I'm a goon," said Mrs. Grubert.

"Does that warm room remind you of anything, Mr. Grubert?"

"Sure, my mother's womb," admitted Grubert. "Only the food is better here."

"Hi, Gloria," said Swineherder. He slapped her on the back. "Sorry I'm late."

"I hadn't noticed."

"This is a guy I found in the woods. He wants to sign up."

Mrs. Swineherder smiled at Haley. "That will be one hundred dollars for this twenty-four hour session. Actually we're getting a late start, for reasons I won't go into. You'll be cheated out of nearly a half hour. I hope you won't mind getting only 23.5 hours of therapy

"You won't get any dessert, either," said Grubert.

"It's obvious this is not a young man who sits around stuffing his face with strudel," said Mrs. Grubert.

Haley grinned at them all. "I'm sure even twelve hours with all of you will do me a world of good." He took out his wallet.

"Your name is?" asked Mrs. Swineherder, taking the money.

"Haley. James Haley."

"Oh, really?" She had been moving the bills toward a breast pocket, but now she rolled them and fit them into an empty space on her cartridge belt. "I'm Gloria Swineherder. Raleigh you already know. The other participants in our trek are Mr. and Mrs. Grubert, Mr. and Mrs. Heckleton and Mr. Creech."

"Now it's truly out of whack," complained Heckleton. "Now it's really many more guys than dolls. Five to three."

"You're thinking of some other kind of encounter,"

said Mrs. Heckleton. "You don't get to swap part-
ners here."

"I'm always hoping," said her husband.

"What you'd really like, you'd like to see me de-
voured by some wild beast."

"No, I wouldn't have to see it. I could only hear
it in the far off distance or even read about it the
next day in a newspaper and I'd· be happy."

Mrs. Heckleton turned to Gloria Swineherder.
"Twenty-four hours in the woods, I don't care how
tough your therapy, it's not going to help this one."

Heckleton said, "You could be married to one of
these other guys. To this little butterball who's got
hot pants for strudel. Or this quiet Creech, who
looks very much like a blazing faggot to me. This
new guy I haven't figured out yet."

"Another one of your famous snap judgments."

"No one gets along in this world," said the slim,
pale Creech. "Mating, pairing off of any kind is ri-
diculous, not to mention revolting. Yet anyone sensitive enough to rebel against the mad patterns of
our culture is labeled odd."

"You talk like a faggot, too," said Heckleton.

Mrs. Swineherder had drawn her husband away
from the group during this exchange and was talking quietly to him. Haley looked beyond them and
made out the chateau's spires and towers, dull gray
in the noon sun, about a quarter mile uphill. Mrs.
Swineherder beckoned to him.

"Yes?"

She said, "Mr. Haley, we neglected to have you
fill out a few release forms, we did. A simple for-

mality to avoid law suits and ill feelings. If you'll step into Tent B with Raleigh for a few minutes."

"I thought you were going to do it," said Swineherder.

"No, you."

"Okay, Gloria. Come along, Haley." He led Haley to the second tent and held the flap aside for him.

Haley moved quickly to the left once inside, but he still took most of the force of the blows from behind.

"She always makes me handle this kind of unpleasantness," he heard Swineherder mutter. He slumped.

XIX

HALEY RAISED his head from the Oriental rug, snorted dust and dander out of his nose. A salmon colored husky dog yawned close to him, licked at his face. Using the friendly dog, Haley boosted himself to a sitting position. Behind the dark wood desk he'd been sprawled in front of Haley saw a bald white-bearded old man. Haley massaged the reachable bones of his upper spine and said, "Dr. Hocktigon?"

The old man moved one hand up in fluttering

short jerks and began fondling one of the ivory elephants on his desk top. "Ach, no," he said in a slow, wowing voice. "Dot's not me, mine friend. Der doctor is offer . . ." His voice ran down, rattled and bumped to a stop. His hand slow motioned, in stop time jerks, toward someplace behind Haley. The bearded old man came up out of his heavy wood chair and his whole body fell in the direction of his thrust hand.

"You're not up on the psychiatric movement and its history," said Dr. Hocktigon. He was sitting at the other side of the room in a blue glass chair that was shaped like an abstract dove.

Rubbing his neck, Haley said, "That's Sigmund Freud?"

"Dot's I'm," growled the android, as its head slid across the desk and scattered ivory pieces and pewter mugs.

After the Freud robot had hit the floor, Dr. Hocktigon said, "A very good replica of Dr. Freud, yes. My parents bought him for me when I was quite young and I've kept him ever since."

Haley said, "He's in need of repairs."

"Dodgast der dadrat," buzzed Freud, his whiskers and the thick rug muffling his rundown voice.

"I never allow him to be tampered with," explained Hocktigon. "Except to have a new suit made for him now and then. I have several very fine Viennese suit patterns, ranging from 1895 to 1930. I like him best in the styles of the 1920s. It's fun to dress him up."

Haley leaned against the desk. "Do you have Penny Duncan here?"

"No." Dr. Hocktigon was a small, grizzled man. His clothes, his hair, his face were mixtures of black and gray. This office was small and cluttered with glass doored bookcases and trophy shelves, heavy wooden tables and old leather chairs. Hocktigon had a white paper bag between his knees.

"Where is she?"

"You have our relationship reversed," said Dr. Hocktigon. "It is I who am to question you. You carelessly gave Gloria Swineherder your real name."

"I thought it might speed up my getting in here," said Haley. "Save me from having to outwit your alarm systems and robot dogs."

Hocktigon nodded. "I see. Perhaps, though, it also indicates stupidity," he said. On a brass hatrack behind him hung several straitjackets. "Certainly it takes away something of the element of surprise. Your actions could even be unwittingly self-destructive, could they not?"

"That's going to depend on the outcome."

The doctor made a smiling sound, opened the paper sack and lifted out a carrot wrapped in a doily. "Gloria served these at dinner last evening and I begged her for leftovers. Mock carrots." He bit off the tip. "Actually, the very fact you selected the Private Inquiry Office as a profession could be an indication you yearn to get yourself destroyed."

"I've survived, though."

"Until today," said Hocktigon. "That's an old joke punchline, as your Penny Deacon would say."

"She was here?"

"Why are you concerned so?"

"I want to find her."

Hocktigon finished the mock carrot and put the bag of them on a round mahogany table at his side. "The basic premise on which I built Vienna West," said the gray and black doctor, "is this: psychiatry got off the track way back at the beginning of the 20th Century." His small hands circled in the air like abstract doves. "Ah, but in Vienna, in Vienna nearly a hundred years ago, Haley, how wonderful life must have been. With Sigmund Freud living and working there in his snug house at 19 Berggasse."

"Stop mit dat," said the collapsed Freud android to the husky, who was licking his horn rimmed glasses at the place they touched the left ear.

"So then," continued Dr. Hocktigon, his hands landing on his round little knees, "so then, Haley, Vienna West is my tribute to that wonderful man. A replica, albeit on a small scale, of the grand Old World city where he flourished and where his ideas came to fruition. My belief, Haley, is that if you give a patient the benefit of Freud's pioneering thought while the selfsame patient is in a very good, though small, replica of Freud's own magic home town, then that patient will be helped." He side-looked at the bag of mock carrots. "Should I have another? No, best not."

"What about Lady Day?"

"Oh, one more won't hurt." The doctor took up

the sack and selected another carrot from within. "Lady Day, Haley, shares my dream."

"Which dream? Are you planning to kill all the prominent men in the Frisco Enclave area, too?"

"Gloria fashions these delightful things from a substance called marzipan, mixed with blackberry cordial and harmless food coloring. Wonderful," said Hocktigon. "No, the dream I have is to build a more elaborate Vienna. Actually—this is confidential, Haley—I'd like to build a one-for-one replica. Full scale. Wouldn't that be something?"

"Why don't you just buy the real Vienna and have it shipped over?"

"This will be more fun, building from scratch. I have all the plans. Street maps, individual building plans. Took me years to collect. Lady Day, who, by the way, has no intention of turning into a mass murderer, will help me fund my bigger and better Vienna."

"What is her intention, then?"

"Simply to kill a few hundred of the key people in your S.F. Enclave government and business hierarchy. Then she'll take over, using the army she's building, and rule. When she does I'll get the co-operation I haven't been able to get from the wishy-washy government of the moment. She'll owe me plenty of cooperation for the help I've given her."

"You help by acting as recruiter and inquisitor?"

"Freud," said Dr. Hocktigon, wiping marzipan flakes from his gray mouth, "lived during the aftermath of the first industrial revolution. There have been many technological upheavals since then, as you are probably aware. Fortunately for science, even the collapse of the United States of America did not cripple the progress of technology, nor completely slow the thrust ahead. Building on, and updating Freud, I have constructed a number of highly proficient psychiatric machines and mechanisms."

"Which you used on Penny."

Hocktigon gestured at a modern metal door behind him. "Would you like to see the interrogation room?"

"I have a hunch I can't refuse."

"That's a perceptive conclusion." A faint beeping commenced above and to his right. "Excuse me." He left his bird shaped chair and opened a high cabinet. A large vidphone screen showed. "Dr. Hocktigon here. Yes?"

The face of a handsome forty-two year old blonde woman snapped onto the phone viewer. "Well, Jackie?"

"In awhile, Lily."

The portion of the woman that showed was naked. "I'm going to be angry, Jackie. I'm going to work myself into a snit. I'm going to rip these rose colored sheets to shreds and tatters. I'm going to throw and strew the goosedown pillows all about the boudoir. I'm going to pile all your oil paintings in the middle of the Armenian rug and dance on them."

"You're angry, Lily, and I understand. I'll be up there with you in not more than an hour," Hocktigon promised the handsome woman.

"Who's there with you?"

"A patient, Lily."

"Let me get a good look at her."

"It's a man."

"I want to see him and hear him talk."

After a moment Hocktigon motioned Haley closer. "Say hello to Lily."

"Hello, Lily," said Haley at the high phone. "You're the other woman, huh?"

"What?" said the undressed Lily.

"Jack here told me he had two broads living here in the chateau and I could have the one he was tired of."

"Jackie, you . . ."

"This man is a patient, Lily. A *mental* patient. He has delusions."

"Stop teasing this nice lady, Jack," said Haley. "Let's get the party started."

"What party?" demanded Lily.

"Oh oh," said Haley. "I guess it was only nurses you invited. My mistake, Jack."

"Jackie, are you up to your old tricks? You promised me I was to be your once and future mistress."

"Lily, calm yourself. Pay no attention to this man. He's goofy. His goofiness makes him lie."

"Well, I'm going to find out." Lily vanished from the screen and it turned black.

"That wasn't smart, Haley," said Dr. Hocktigon. "I have you under my thumb. Making trouble for me with the woman I love at the moment isn't going to do you any good."

Someone knocked at the thick dark wood door at the other end of the office. "She dresses fast," said Haley.

"Who is it?" shouted Hocktigon.

"Nurse Newberry."

"Say that again."

"Nurse Newberry. What's wrong?"

Hocktigon unlocked and opened the door narrowly. "So it is you."

"I've been taking elocution lessons for when we take over this half of the state and I become press secretary," said the orange haired nurse. "Have I spoiled the basic pleasant quality of my voice?"

"No, no, my dear, I was merely being very careful. What is it?"

The nurse held up the large silver covered dish she was carrying. "This is the new vegetable surprise Gloria Swineherder sent over this morning, remember? You said you wanted it for lunch."

"Nurse Newberry, you shouldn't break in when I'm grilling a prisoner."

She glanced around the little doctor. "Oh, he's the straight Penny fell for. Hi."

"You can bring that in," Haley told the girl. "We're in no hurry."

"It'll get cold if you don't eat it soon." The orange haired girl pushed into the office.

"Very well. Place it on the desk," said the doctor. "I sometimes doubt, Nurse Newberry, you'll fit into any very exalted position in the new government."

"Don't say that. Gee, here I am working part time as a nurse so as to have a cover role and I'm going to night school and I'm in the Mankill, Inc. movement. Boy, some days I have to get by on less than six hours sleep." She hefted the big polished serving dish and placed it on the desk. "My, Mr. Freud fell over again."

"You can pick him up later."

The chunky orange haired girl went down on her knees next to the motionless android. "Gee, I hate to see a sweet old man stretched out on the floor. It's probably because of my unfortunate relationship with my own father, wouldn't you think?"

"Yes, yes." Hocktigon's hand rattled the knob of the door. "This is an android, Nurse Newberry, not actually a real old man. It does not hurt him in the least to be on the floor, especially since I am too busy, much too busy, to pick him up. You can go now."

"Bad dog," said the nurse. "Look what he's gone and done, Dr. Hocktigon. He's bitten off poor Mr. Freud's ear. Give that back, doggie."

The salmon colored husky slithered backwards under the desk, growling quietly and negatively. He held the android's synthetic flesh ear in his teeth.

"We have spare ears, Nurse Newberry, plenty of them. Please go now."

"Doggie, doggie, nice doggie." The girl lowered herself to her stomach and stretched one arm under the big desk. "Give me, give me the ear, doggie. Doggie doesn't want to keep Mr. Freud's nice ear. No, no, doggie would rather have a nice puppy biscuit. Come on, doggie."

"Ho, ho," cried Lily, pushing into the office and waving a blaster pistol over her head. "Look at this fine kettle of fish, Jackie."

"Calm yourself, Lily."

She was wearing only a short terry robe. "Look at this pretty picture. My own Jackie cavorting with a dirty old man and a fat dyke. My, my."

"Give me the gun, Lily," said Hocktigon. "You are misunderstanding, my dear. Give me the gun and go back to the master bedroom. I'll join you just as soon as possible."

"You promised that two hours ago and I'm still cooling my heels." Lily slammed the wood door closed with her angry buttocks and pointed the blaster more directly at the doctor. "Can't you stand to be with me in the daylight?"

"Right," said Haley. "She doesn't look anything as bad as you said, Jack. I'll go ahead with the deal. You get the nurse and I get Lily. Okay by me. How about you, Lil?"

"Oh, bad doggie," said the orange haired nurse, now half under the desk. "Let go of nurse's thumb."

"Baby talk," said Lily. "Really, Jackie, I thought you'd gotten over your fetish for youth. You're forty-nine, after all."

"Forty-eight," corrected Dr. Hocktigon. "Please, Lily, ignore what you see here. Particularly ignore Mr. Haley. He's a very neurotic young man."

"He's cute," said Lily.

"Let's open the party favors," suggested Haley, "and get things rolling."

"What party favors?" asked Lily.

"Jack had the redhead bring in some stuff. Hidden in that fancy dish there, Lil."

"Jackie, are you on something again? Are you taking those sex pills again?"

"No, no, Lily. You must relax."

"Ow, ow, bad doggie."

"Jack, you ought to level with her," said Haley, edging over to the desk. "Let her see what you've got in there."

"Yes." Lily bounded behind the desk and lifted the lid. Six stuffed cabbages jumped up into her face and she screamed and let go of the pistol.

Haley leaped and was over the wide desk in time to catch the falling pistol. "Okay," he said. He nudged Lily with his free fist. "Over to the other side of the office. Sit in the blue chair and shut up."

"You're not as polite as I thought, nor as gentle."

"Go, sit." Haley then poked the still prone Nurse Newberry with his foot. "You, crawl out on my side and then go sit next to Lil."

"What about Mr. Freud's ear?"

Haley didn't reply. To the small black and gray Dr. Hocktigon he said, "Now, let's get back to our earlier conversation. Where's Penny Deacon?"

"You really do like her, huh?" Nurse Newberry emerged in front of him.

"Sit down and remain silent," Haley ordered. When she was seated next to Lily, Haley continued, "Okay Hocktigon. Where?"

"Well," said the doctor.

Haley squeezed the trigger of the blaster and six bound volumes of the *Psychological Review* and an ivory bison sizzled into dust to the immediate left of Hocktigon's head. "No more bullshit," said Haley.

"Tell him, Jackie," said the paling Lily.

"She is not here, Haley," said Hocktigon, his thin gray lips close together. "Believe me. A group of Lady Day's Mankill girls have taken her away. They left early this morning, after I had finished questioning her. She's with the other hostages now."

"Okay, and where is that?"

"Monterey," said Hocktigon.

"That's right," said Nurse Newberry.

Hocktigon said, "They plan a mass execution. Three political prisoners and Penny Deacon. At high noon tomorrow."

"At what location?"

"During the Monterey Mechanical Jazz Festival," said the doctor. "Tomorrow will be the final day of that."

"Lady's biggest public killing yet," said Nurse Newberry. "It's going to scare the daylights out of the straights."

"Lily," said Haley, "get three of those restraining jackets off the hat rack over there."

"Whatever for?"

"To restrain you and Nurse Newberry and Dr. Hocktigon until some kind of cops can get here. Move, now."

When the three, aided by Haley, were all straitjacketed, he said, "You, Hocktigon, I want in the next room. Through the metal door."

"Are you going to do something awful to Jackie?" asked the immobile Lily.

"No, I'm only going to use some of his interrogating equipment to find out a few more things, including how to get myself safely out of the chateau," said Haley. "And I want to confirm what he's already told me."

"I was telling you the truth," said Dr. Hocktigon. He was.

XX

HALEY, having parked his borrowed ambulance, came walking down the crowded street leading to the fair grounds. He noticed the sheriff of Monterey standing with one booted foot on the body of an unconscious local cop, his chubby hand poised over his holster.

"No, no, kids," the sheriff was saying. "I'd take that as a definite violation of our agreement."

Two dozen young people were shuffling in half circles around him and the fallen local. "We just only want to set him on fire for a little bit," pleaded a thin blond boy.

"No immolations, no conflagrations," pointed out the sheriff. "Everybody agreed on that. Now if it was just up to me, kids, I'd say okey dokey, light him up for a couple of minutes. So long as you snuffed him out before he got seriously burned. See, but I got the city fathers to think about and a lot of other prominent people in the area."

"Frick the prominent people," said a silver haired girl. "We thought you meant we couldn't set ourselves on fire."

"I knocked him down," said the blond boy. "I don't see why I don't get to do what I want with him."

The sheriff gave a short, clipped sigh. "Look now, suppose I let you give him a hotfoot. Would that satisfy you for awhile and help clear the air?"

"What the frack is a hot foot?" asked the silver haired girl. She squeezed her bare left breast absently, her face puckering at the large plump sheriff.

"You know, I think you kids nowadays miss half the fun we had in my day. A hotfoot is where you stick a match in a guy's shoe without his knowing and then you light it."

The two dozen milling young people made groaning sounds. "Then what?" asked the silvered girl.

"Well, nothing. The guy yowls and hops around and everybody has a good laugh."

"Come on," insisted the blond boy. "Let us set him on fire, why don't you?"

The stunned local cop sat up, licked his lips, rubbed at his sandy hair. "The heck," he said in a dry voice. "The heck you will."

"See," complained the silver haired girl, "all this talk and now he's awake and that's not any fun setting him on fire if he's wide awake."

Haley pushed on through the crowds and along the hot afternoon street. Aluminum arbors had been erected all around the fair grounds. Two stories high and topped with light strip pennants. The name

Monterey Mechanical Jazz Festival flashed and blinked and glowed at a dozen places on the façade, in varying colors and sizes.

Paying his $10 admission, Haley worked down through the hundreds of people who were loitering or wandering outside the boardwalled oval housing the entertainment. He got tangled with a freckled family group. Father, mother, and two lean under-twenty children, one boy and one girl.

"He does understand," the mother was telling the boy, who swayed gently, eyes closed.

"Sure, why else am I here?" The father smiled and it spread all over his face, ending in the lines beneath his eyes and across his sunburned forehead. "I understand you, Boober."

"Um," replied the boy.

The daughter grimaced. "Holy bloody Jesus," she said in a pinched voice. "For the love of the sweet god damn Virgin Mary, don't keep calling him Boober. He's full grown."

Her father said, "Four years at a convent school and all you learn is how to blaspheme."

"Oh, great bloody wounds of our precious Lord and Savior," said the girl. "Why can't you recognize his adulthood and autonomy?"

"Why would I be here if I didn't?"

"Yes, Marcella," said her mother. "We're really trying, honey. Let's go inside and enjoy this music, if we can."

"Um um," said Boober.

Haley made his way clear and headed down a scruffy grass hill, weaving through sharp elbows and knees, narrow backs. Two overweight Negro girls danced briefly with him. "Anything you want?" asked one.

"Not that I can think of," he answered, dancing free.

"We got pills, booze, THC, gadgets, bizarre sex," offered the black girl.

Haley grinned and the two girls turned away. He went further downhill and around a grove of trees and tripped over La Penna.

The curly PIO man was kneeling lazily beside a long pale olive colored girl who was wearing only a pair of lemon yellow riding pants. La Penna was fully dressed in quiet civilian clothes. "Hey, Jim," said La Penna, his bushy moustache rising up as he smiled. "Como está?"

"Working?"

La Penna got up, slapped at the grass stains on his knees. "Tell you later. Hey, I want you to meet this girl."

The girl had a shady, high boned beauty. A slightly nasty smile. "Buenos dias, gringito," she said.

"Don't act now, you silly bimbo," La Penna said. "This is a real friend of mine. Jim, this is Mama Cholo."

"Hello," said the girl, sitting up. "You don't know Mech Jazz, right?"

Haley said, "Sure, you're Mama Cholo and Her Tijuana Trash. You're playing the festival with your group."

"Bonito," said the girl. "This one, Gorditio here,

he knows nothing of my career until he met me last night. Es verdad, cabrito?"

"You ought to see her act," said La Penna. "She plays this gigantic amplified guitar. It hides her chest too much, but she plays it well. And her brother plays an aluminum marimba and they got two garbage trucks and a street sweeping robot working with them. They play and sing, the trucks crash and the robot tap dances and they never miss a beat. It's an experience."

"We're very good," said Mama Cholo, "but we like to keep a little peon image in the act for gringitos like this one."

La Penna bent and kissed the girl. "I'll be back with you soon, Mama. I've got to talk to my friend."

A few yards from her they stopped. Haley said, "Tomorrow at noon Lady Day's people are supposed to stage a flash execution here. With the mayor of San Arturo and two other politicians. And probably with Penny."

"That last part I didn't know. I came here on a tip Mama is involved in the prostitution business, which she is," said La Penna. "I also got the Mankill girls spotted and I think I can guess where they have Penny and the others."

"Dr. Hocktigon didn't know what cover they were using," said Haley. "Where are they?"

"I figured you might track them here," La Penna told him. "I was going to wait till sundown and if you didn't show, call Chief McGuinness. Let's go inside the arena and you can confirm my identification."

"That's where they are?"

"Yeah, two of them are performing right now," said La Penna. "As the Mechanical Jazz Half Girl Quartet. Mama knows about them, but not much else about Lady Day. Did this Hocktigon tell you where Lady Day's ultimate headquarters is?"

"No. She apparently doesn't trust any guy enough to let him know that."

La Penna guided Haley onto one of the wood ramps leading into the entertainment area. Haley asked, "What about Penny?"

"These broads got a big old land bus they use. Windows are blacked over in the back half. Be a good place to hide people. They've been sneaking food in there from the refreshment areas."

Only five of the seven round platform stages were in use for the afternoon mechanical jazz concert. The raised platforms sprawled across the local fair ground field, surrounded by sharply rising temporary bleachers. Music and shouting, mechanical noise and enthusiastic cheering shot straight up into the waning afternoon. La Penna took a position down on the stage of the field, squatting among young people. Haley edged in next to him. Close to his ear La Penna said, "I don't know the names of all these groups playing, but the one we're interested in is on the third stage from the left. The two broads with the pinball machine and automatic piano."

"Hey, peanut brain," shouted a Chinese girl next to La Penna, "don't talk during the music."

"I was only trying to identify the musicians for

my older friend," said La Penna, smiling. "You're a very pretty girl."

"What?"

"I said you're not bad looking," shouted La Penna, "but you seem to have a mean streak."

The girl heard him, nodded. "Thanks, but I don't ball guys with moustaches. It's a quirk maybe, but that's how it is. Could you shave it off?"

La Penna shook his head. "No. Besides, you wouldn't really like me if I did. The guy has got to be the dominant one in any relation."

The Chinese girl said, "You may be right. See, I'm in the process of getting myself normalized by taking a course in psychotherapy via pay television. I'm only up to lesson six."

"We'll get together when you graduate."

The girl leaned across and poked Haley. "I don't ball guys so skinny either, but I might make an exception. You're rather starkly attractive."

Haley was watching the girls La Penna had pointed out. He grinned without looking at the Chinese girl.

"Yes, that skeletal grin intrigues me," she decided. "I can tell you who all the musicians and groups are if that'll help you feel at home here."

"Not necessary," said Haley. The black girl playing soprano saxophone was one of the four who'd taken Penny.

"On this stage nearest us is Lorenzo Killdozer and His Tribe. That's Lorenzo on the jack hammer and his common law wife is up next to him smashing the piano with a fire ax. The kid on the drill press is Jimmy Chan. I went to high school with him. The guitar and the drums, those are androids playing them. Andies I find creepy," she said. "Again, I'm willing to admit a few more doses of psychotherapy may change or at least modify my attitudes." She paused to tug once at La Penna's moustache. "That big sensual looking spade on platform six is Texas Soww with his New Washboard Rhythm Kings. I'm not sure why they call themselves that. I suppose it has something to do with all the laundromat machines he uses in his act. The guy sitting on the mangle and playing the mouth harp is new to me. Hey, look, Texas is stripping and throwing his clothes in that washing machine. See, he can play the trumpet at the same time. That would be interesting in bed, wouldn't it?"

"Not as interesting as a moustache."

Haley said, "Let's get out and take a look at their bus."

La Penna patted the girl's hand. "We'll meet again. Patience."

Suds began to erupt out of Texas Soww's washer and the Chinese girl turned in mid goodbye to watch.

XXI

Twilight began to flow into the grassy fields where the musician's vehicles were parked. Standing in among oak trees, La Penna said to Haley, "There's the two from the concert going into their bus."

"Yeah," said Haley, his eyes narrow, watching the big gray land bus two hundred yards down the slope. "Which means all five of the Lady Day girls are in there now, if you counted right."

La Penna said, "You can trust me on counting women." He shook something into his palm from a yellow tube.

"What's that?" asked Haley, noticing the motion of La Penna's hand moving up.

"Huh?" La Penna looked at the two scarlet spansules approaching his mouth. "What am I doing, eating part of my disguise?" He dropped the spansules back in the tube, pocketed it. "Nerve pills. I must be really jumpy to start to take those things myself." He fussed with his moustache, shook his head. "Must be contagious, Jim. I caught it from you, I guess. You should relax."

Haley frowned at his partner. "Look, Joel," he began. He stopped, grinned a brief grin. "Yes, I am jumpy. I'm worried about Penny. I want to get her out of there."

"We will. You like her quite a bit?"

Haley nodded. "Let's get back to the nearest refreshment area for a minute."

"That's okay you get to like a girl you meet on a case," said La Penna, falling in beside Haley. "I do myself. I screw a lot of women in the line of duty, Jim, but sometimes I also get to like them. Not love maybe, not anything you'd want to build a house and put down a lawn over, but real authentic affection."

"I suppose," said Haley as they neared the still sparsely frequented refreshment area, "I'm thinking it's not professional."

"Some guys can lock in permanently," said La Penna. "They can go on grinning and bribing their way through life till they fall over dead or are done in. Other guys get sidetracked now and then, which is how you grow and flourish."

"I'm sidetracked, then," said Haley. He stopped alongside a mansize soft drink machine labeled *Mojo Kola! 6 Lucky Flavors!* Haley genuflected next to the crimson machine. "We're going to borrow this." He fritzed the alarm lock, picked it and unplugged the big soft drink dispenser. "We should be able to heft it down to the bus. You armed?"

"Pistol. You?"

"Pistol." Haley slipped his blaster out of his shoulder holster and tucked it into his waist band. "This Mojo machine is now a new instrument being delivered to the quartet from a Miss Newberry of Vienna West."

"Trojan horse," said La Penna, shifting his own pistol to a more quickly reachable position.

"Only we extemporize more." Haley grunted once and got a grip on the topside of the machine.

La Penna grappled with the base of the Mojo Kola machine and the two PI men got it upended and into a horizontal position. "Some doctors will dispute it," said La Penna. "But screwing is good exercise. I owe most of my incredible strength to that."

They carried the machine downhill, through the darkening trees, brought it slowly right up to the Mankill girls' bus. La Penna was in the lead and he groaned and then reached up and rapped on the bus door.

"Set it down for awhile," Haley said.

They eased the soft drink machine to the thick grass and then La Penna knocked again. "Hey, girls. Wake up. We're on a tight schedule."

The bus door hissed open halfway. A lean black girl swung out of the driver's seat and then came down the three rubberized steps to the opening. "What?"

"Open the doors wide, lady," said La Penna. "The Galileo Moving Company is here."

Haley did not recognize this member of the Lady Day group.

"Go away, schmuck," said the girl. She wore one plain gold ring in her pierced left ear.

"Glad to, lady. All you got to do is sign for this mother and we'll unload it on you and haul out."

"We come over from Vienna West with this," said Haley. "The girl there told us it was a rush. An emergency."

"What girl, schlep?"

La Penna scratched his chin, then his moustache ends. "What was that broad's name? Newberg?"

"Newberry, wasn't it?" said Haley.

La Penna swung one foot up and rested it on the red machine. "See, lady, we got a rate schedule that goes day time, time and a half, overtime and golden time. Right about ten minutes ago we crossed into golden time. But this Miss Newbunny told us to spare no expense in getting this special mechanical jazz equipment to you girls."

"Newberry," corrected the black girl. She stepped down one step more.

"She told us," added Haley, "you had to have this for your performance tomorrow."

The girl came to the bottom step and stretched out a tan booted foot, kicking at the soft drink machine. "We weren't anticipating . . ." She started to say. "Well, okay, schmucks. Leave it right there. Goodbye."

"No, no," said La Penna. "We got to deliver it inside the bus. That's the agreement we signed with Newpenny."

"Newberry," said the black girl. "You can't."

"Apparently you aren't up on the rules and regulations laid down by the San Francisco Enclave Motor Carrier Act of 1989," said La Penna. He bent and took hold of his end of the machine.

Haley lifted the rear and they pushed the front end of the big machine up into the bus.

"Wait, schlep," said the angry girl. "Now, see, you got that dumb piece of junk wedged."

"I thought this was your vocation, lady," said La Penna. "Playing guitars and machinery and jumping up and down. You seem disdainful of the tools of your trade." He swung with his shoulder and the machine lurched ten inches further through the half open door.

The girl backed up the steps. "Get that unstuck, schmuck."

"It won't budge, lady," La Penna told her. "You better open the doors all the way wide."

"Okay," said the girl. "Hold it now, don't do any more dumb things until I get the door undone." She slammed her narrow buttocks onto the driver's seat and yanked at the door release handle.

The doors sighed and opened full. La Penna charged upwards and he and Haley came fully into the bus with the horizontal Mojo Kola machine between them. "Now where do we set this, lady?"

The bus interior was divided in the middle by heavy black metal walling. In the visible portion there were only two more of the Lady Day girls, the Negro girl who worked in the mechanical jazz group and a pale blonde with short cropped hair. The blonde was the only one of the three wearing black clothes.

"You crumb bum," said the black girl at the wheel. "I told you and I told you to leave it outside."

La Penna and Haley proceeded further into the

bus, carrying the heavy machine toward the partition and the other two girls, who were seated on either side of its narrow black door.

The second Negro girl said, "Hold it, fellows. Put that right down there and that will be fine." The machine kept her from getting an unobstructed view of Haley.

The angry girl left the seat and came up behind Haley. She caught his arm and said, "Schmuck, why don't you listen when a person tells you something?"

Haley found the machine was wide enough to rest on the arms of the bus seat and that it rested high enough to block the other two girls' view of him. He quietly turned and clipped the girl twice on the chin. "Don't touch that, lady," he said.

The girl fell to her knees and then tumbled over sideways, half in the aisle and half in a pile of uniforms, belts, decorative braiding.

"Oh boy," said Haley. "She got herself a bad electrical shock or something from touching the power unit on this machine here."

"There goes our good record with the insurance company," said La Penna.

"What?" the other black girl rushed to La Penna, then hunched by him and came under the machine and out at Haley's end of it. When she bent to examine the knocked out girl, Haley gave her three quick chops to the side of her neck. She gasped once and passed out, falling just to the left of the first girl.

"Nobody else had better come back here," said

Haley. "Something is really going blooey with this machine. It's knocking out girls right and left."

"What are you talking about?" The blonde was standing in front of La Penna. "That gadget isn't even plugged in."

La Penna made an agreeing sound and moved his two hands in different ways, clapping one over the blonde's mouth and drawing out his pistol and showing it to her with the other.

Haley gathered up belts and cords from the pile of uniforms and tied the angry girl's hands behind her. He gagged her with a sleeve ripped off a jacket and sat her up in one of the worn brown noga seats. He tied and gagged the second girl while La Penna did the same thing with the upright blonde, one handed.

"Hey, ladies," La Penna called out when he was done. "We seem to have something out of the ordinary going on out here." He went quickly sideways to the door in the metal partition and back jumped so he'd be behind it when it opened.

Haley ducked under the soft drink machine, went by the gagged and seated blonde and took a position in the aisle that would hide her from whoever opened the door.

The partition door swung barely open, silently. "What is this?" asked the slim brunette girl standing stiff at the slit.

"Well, this mech jazz machine is supposed to get delivered to somebody in your group," said Haley. "It comes special rush from Vienna West and a Miss Newberry."

"Where's Juanita?"

"There haven't been any introductions yet," Haley told her. "But if Juanita is one of the girls who was out here, I'm afraid she's been seriously hurt. Injured by a malfunction in this Mojo Kola machine."

"You stupid bastard," said the dark haired girl. "What have you done to poor Nita?" She straight-armed the door wide and ran for Haley. He side-stepped and the girl saw the blonde. The brunette started to turn her head and cry out. Haley caught her and stopped her.

From behind him a slightly nasal woman's voice said, "Let her go and turn this way with your . . . oof."

Haley proceeded to tie and gag the brunette with parts of uniforms. When he looked behind him he saw La Penna arranging the fifth and last Lady Day girl in a bus seat.

When he had her bound and muffled La Penna said, "Want to step to the rear of the bus?"

"Five girls was all, huh?"

"Far as I know."

The door was now half open. No one else had emerged. Haley nodded his head once and went to the doorway. He booted it full open and charged in. Four people were in the darkened last half of the bus, tied with baling wire and gagged with medical tape and gauze.

One of them was Penny. Haley went first to her. She was alive and this caused him to laugh, out loud and unexpectedly.

XXII

PENNY THRUST her hands deep in the pockets of her borrowed duffel coat and walked toward the end of the rundown wooden pier. The dark ocean was topped with cold gray fog. A wind came up across the moon white sand and rattled the false vines tangled across the front of a boarded up seafood restaurant. "We're always alone by the ocean," she said to Haley. She took his hand. "Always by some defunct building or other."

"There's a lot of that going around," Haley said.

Penny said, "You looked pleased a couple of hours ago."

"I was," he answered. "I still am."

"But now," said the girl, "you're thinking you have to go on and find Lady Day."

Haley leaned against a secure piling. "Yeah, I still have that to do."

"Your office, your Private Inquiry Office, and the Intelligence and Investigation Office," said the lean, dark haired girl, "they'll be here in Monterey soon and they'll take charge of the Lady Day girls that your friend La Penna and the local cops are watching back at the fair grounds. They'll question everybody, one way or another, and they'll find out what they want to know. Including the whereabouts of Lady Day."

"Probably," said Haley.

"Those machines of Hocktigon's," she said, "really, they really work quite well." She brought his hand up and touched it to her chin. "You don't know much about me, Jim. The more you'll find out, the less you'll like me."

Haley moved his knobby hand, fingers spread, up and rested it on her cheek. "Nobody I've run into on this assignment gets along very well," he said. "Do you realize that, that most people are always arguing with each other?" He stopped, laughed. "That's obvious, isn't it? I didn't mean to make it sound like something profound."

"Nothing wrong with being obvious," said the girl, smiling her intricate smile. "Or profound either. Right now you think I'm exceptional and I feel that way about you and you don't want a lot of arguing and talking getting in the way. I know."

"Yes," said Haley.

"Except you're liking me on not enough," said the girl. "Not enough data, insufficient evidence. I'm really not too admirable."

"I like you because of what you are at the moment," Haley said. "Look, Penny, I'd have to be kind of dimwitted not to understand what links Lady Day's girls together. So when you were in the group you slept with someone, one of the girls, and now that fact is supposed to drive me off."

Penny inhaled and eased away from him, fisted her hands back in the pockets of her knee length coat. "Yes, that's right. One particular girl. That's how I got persuaded to join the movement. Try anything once. That's an old punchline, too. I changed my mind about that, about the girl, about what Lady Day was up to. But still it all has happened. Sure, you 'can talk about things, Jim, but I don't know if you can accommodate them inside yourself."

"What I meant about nobody getting along," said Haley. "I meant we didn't have to play that. We might skip over it."

"Might," said Penny. "You're not optimistic either."

"I'm more optimistic than I've been," Haley told her. He laughed. "I take that as a good sign."

Penny turned from the black ocean and watched him. "Well," she said. "So do I. I don't know, a lot of things have to be mended. I think we're both going to be a little hesitant and a little grudging about keeping on with each other. Yes, I guess I'm optimistic, too." She drew one hand out and stroked at her cheek. "I can tell you where Lady Day is, where her hideaway is. You can follow through and finish this job. And then . . ."

"Okay," said Haley.

"I heard things while they've had me here at the festival," said Penny. "They let slip, amid threats about what an example they were going to make of me, where Lady Day keeps her headquarters. There's a place down at Big Sur, not that far away."

Haley finally said, "Do you know the location?"

"She's using an old place on a hill above the ocean," said the girl. "There's supposed to be a tower, a stone tower and a large house, several wooded acres. The whole thing supposedly belonged to a famous old California poet. I don't know his name, but the house is called Stallion's Reach."

"I've heard of it," said Haley. "How many Mankill people are there with her?"

"A hundred at least," answered Penny. "She's heavily but unobtrusively guarded."

"By noon tomorrow," said Haley, "if not sooner, Lady Day'll learn things have gone wrong here in Monterey. We should get inside Stallion's Reach before then."

"If you had a mobile computer, you could drive right in."

"Had what?"

Penny said, "Early today, when I first got brought into that damn bus, there were some other Lady Day girls there. Five of them. They said Lady had sent them out to round up a mobile computer. She wants to have one at Stallion's Reach."

"Did those five girls have a lead on one?"

"I think so," Penny said. "They were on their way up the coast, toward Frisco, to check out a report on somebody who had one. Some private party, not any government thing."

"Jacovetti," said Haley.

"Who?"

"William Francis Jacovetti, former Director of the Federal Bureau of Investigation. He has a motel and a mobile computer."

"He should be content."

"I wonder if we can do the Trojan horse twice."

"I didn't know you'd done it once."

Haley said, "I'll call Jacovetti and alert him, in case he hasn't been approached yet. Then we can get up there, if the damn computer is still safe, and borrow the thing."

"I'll come with you," said Penny. "I assume that's what you mean by we."

Haley smiled at the girl. "Now that you mention it, I guess it is."

XXIII

THROUGH THE cold rain came the sound and flash of machine guns and then the keening crackle of blaster rifles. Haley slowed his borrowed land car and said, "Looks like the Mankill girls have found the mobile computer." Braking, he swung off the road and into a field bordering a pine forest.

Penny frowned, straining to see through the dark and rain. "Somebody just shot off the vacancy sign." She reached over, her hand pressing the hollow of his arm. "You should maybe call in for help."

"When we go up against Lady Day herself I'll have help from I&I." He stretched and carefully took his borrowed blaster rifle from the rear seat of the small car. "But not now. How many girls did Lady Day send on this job?"

"Five," said Penny. "One of them is six foot two."

"You stay here, Penny." Haley put his pistol in her hand. "I'm going down through the woods and see how close I can get to the G-Man Motel."

"They'll shoot you before you can shoot them," said the girl. "At least, five to one would seem to indicate that."

"I'm not going to shoot anybody," Haley told her. "I'm only going to incapacitate a few of the girls."

"They said you hit an old lady with a clock in San Bonito."

"I did." Haley shifted the rifle, leaned and kissed Penny. "Okay, I'll be back."

"I can come along and help."

"No." He eased open the door on his side of the car. "Wait and watch."

Penny said, "I don't like rain much better than earthquakes."

"Those old G-Men down there came three thousand miles for this weather." Haley left the car and began moving quietly through the pines. The rain came in straight falling fat drops, rustling hard and cold down through the branches. A gust of wind came and blew damp pine needles across him.

Haley continued on until he could see the office building and the outer cabins of the former FBI chief's motel. He stopped, crouched. Agent 27 sprang from behind the office and sent a burst of antique machine gun slugs toward a spot five hundred feet below Haley. Two blaster rifles crackled and Agent 27 ducked away safely. Haley walked the darkness and gradually made out two of the Mankill girls bellied down in wild grass. He halted.

Nearer to the office a girl spoke up over a portable bull horn. "We don't want to kill any of you old coots," she announced into the rainy dark. "Throw away those old guns and give up. All we want is your mobile computer."

27, cupping his hands to his mouth apparently, shouted back, "A G-Man never quits."

"Okay, it's your ass in a sling, gramps."

Blaster fire from three rifles hit the ground near the old agent. From behind a cabin another old FBI man, in nightshirt and flannel robe, jumped and fired his machine gun at the place where the two girls were stretched out.

Haley now knew the positions of three Mankill, Inc. girls and two old G-Men. He began stalking. He came at the two nearest girls sideways and silent. Six feet behind them, rifle resting waist high, Haley said, "Okay. Stand up and leave your guns on the ground."

"Darn," said the blonde Lady Day girl, seeing him. She got up, complied.

The other girl, who was fat and six feet tall, got up slower, asking, "Who the crap are you?"

Haley asked the blonde, "Where are the other girls?"

"What other girls?" said the tall one. "We're a couple of lonely stenographers enjoying a friendly turkey shoot."

"You," Haley said to the blonde, "take off your belt and tie your friend's hands behind her."

"You some kind of bizarre night rapist?" asked the fat tall girl.

"No more talking," said Haley.

When he had both the Mankill girls tied and gagged he left them and progressed toward the third. He was still ten feet from her when twin Japanese girls tackled him, took his rifle, and bulldogged him.

"Which branch of the government are you with?" asked one of the Mankill, Inc. twins.

Tied, doubled up in wet brush and thick mud, Haley said, "I'm a freelance commando."

"A wise ass," observed the other Japanese girl. "Shoot him and let's grab that gadget."

"No," said her sister. "He could be somebody important, since he's obviously not an old government detective. We ought to hold on to him, a hostage."

"We don't have orders to take any prisoners. Come on, sis, stand over a little and I'll fry him with my hand blaster."

"I still think we ought to salvage him."

"Okay, reach for it," said a voice from among the pines.

"Now we missed our chance," said the twin who wanted to kill Haley. She threw her pistol down, hitting him on the ear with it.

William Francis Jacovetti, wearing candy stripe pajamas and carrying two .45 automatics, stepped into view. "I was already a past master of commando tactics before you girls were born," he said. "I even have a diploma from the Green Beret school. You probably never heard of them. You should have thought twice before sneaking up on me." He came closer and looked down at Haley. "You're the op from Frisco, aren't you? It's hard to tell from this angle and without my specs."

"Yes," said Haley. "I got two of these Lady Day girls tied up before the twins got me. There should be only one more still loose."

"I got this here talkative one," announced an old agent over the bullhorn.

"That makes five," said Haley. "All there are, according to my information."

Jacovetti swung one gun toward the woods. "Then what about this one?"

Haley got himself half up. "She's with me. Hello, Penny."

Penny stepped tentatively closer. "I decided to come and help anyway. Do you need any?"

"You could help by untying me." The Japanese twins had used a length of plastic clothesline to truss him up.

"Do they really want my old mobile computer?" Jacovetti asked. "Or was that simply a ruse, an excuse to mow us down?"

"Lady Day wants it," said Haley.

Penny bit her tongue slightly as she worked at the knots. "Ask him if you can borrow it."

"Borrow my favorite computer?" Jacovetti's wrinkle doodled old face twitched negatively.

"It's in the interest of law and order," said Haley.

Jacovetti's rain soaked pajamas were blotched to his skin. He worked his forefinger over one of the sticking spots on his lower ribs and said, "Well. Well. Well, okay."

Penny got the last of the knots undone and Haley stood up.

XXIV

PENNY WALKED through the morning grass and handed Haley a cup of coffee. "He says he can make donuts, too," she said.

"Who, Chief McGuinness?"

"No, your borrowed computer." She touched one palm to the bright grass and lowered herself down next to Haley. "He says donuts, crullers, scones and simple fried pastries. There's a place where you can pour in vegetable oil."

"Did he make this coffee?"

"Yes, from real coffee beans. Jacovetti gets them from some old retired Mafia people in Tijuana."

Haley sipped hot coffee, watching the morning light spread through the woods and rolling fields around them. They were near Big Sur. "You feeling okay? You're sure you want to drive the truck in?"

Penny took the cup gently from him and drank. "Yes. You need somebody who can pass as a Mankill driver. It's either me or Buddy Plastino."

A man in a woods colored suit rattled out from the trees, a communications jack inserted in his ear. "Haley," he said, "all the support people are in place."

Haley got the coffee back and finished it. He hunched once and his bones crackled. Rising up, he said, "Okay, Reisberson. Let's get back to the truck, Penny."

"The computer can fry eggs, too," she said, following him. "But not scramble. That FBI must have had some budget. This is a real luxury model computer."

Haley said, "The United States Government always went first cabin." They crossed through the brightening morning and he helped the slim girl up into the computer trailer.

Chief McGuinness of the San Francisco Enclave Intelligence and Investigation Office had both of his hands pressed against the face of the big old fashioned computer. "Get those back in there, will you?" he was saying to the wall wide machine. "I don't want us to roll into Lady Day's stronghold smelling like a lunch wagon." A little compartment in the computer snapped its door open against the pressure of McGuinness' palms. A donut popped out. There were six others, plus a maple bar, at the I&I chief's feet. "Did you hear we're all set, Jim? All the attack personnel are in place. Twenty-five I&I Special Commandos, fifty S.F. Enclave Tactical Cops, and we were lucky enough to get a hundred men from the Voluntary Army at Ft. Ord. Stop that now, you stupid machine."

"You shouldn't start a mission on an empty stomach," the computer warned.

"I already had a cup of your coffee."

"Solid food is what I mean," said the big machine. It fired out one more donut and quit. "How about that? Coconut on top."

"There must be something about me, Jim, which arouses machinery," said Chief McGuinness. "They bristle when I'm in the vicinity. I'm like that—who was it?—Typhoid Mary who made everybody sick. I really have a very negative effect on machines."

"No wonder you have typhoid," said the computer. "The way you skip breakfast. Would you like to see a copy of the Department of Agriculture nutrition chart?"

"No." McGuinness snatched a donut off the metallic floor of the trailer and took an angry bite. "Okay, all right. I'm eating something. Now shut up. You have an important part to play in this subterfuge. Don't go showing off and screwing up our impersonation."

"How can I do that," said the computer. "I really am a computer."

"Well, then stop acting like a short order cook."

Haley said, "We're about ten minutes from Stallion's Reach. Shall we start for there?"

"Yes," said McGuinness. Absently, he took another bite out of the coconut donut. "Miss Deacon, are you prepared?"

Penny smiled and shrugged, her arms rising at her side. "Far as I can tell."

"I'm assuming the passwords and countersigns we

180

got from the Mankill girls are going to work," Mc-
Guinness told her, "and that there are enough girls
stationed down there that nobody will be able to tell
immediately you're not one of them." He glanced at
Haley. "Those Trooz pills seem to work quite well,
Jim."

"Better than slapping them around," said Penny.

"We don't use that sort of technique, Miss Deacon. In fact, I&I hasn't used any sort of physical
persuasion since . . . oh, it must be a good ten years
since we have. Now let's proceed."

Penny patted Haley's shoulder and stepped through
the door at the front of the trailer and into the
cab of the truck. "Listen close when we get to the
gate house. If our entry code isn't the right one
you'll hear me getting shot."

"Easy now," Haley said.

"Be sure and tap on the connecting door if any
of the Mankill girls decide to inspect the computer
before we're inside the stronghold," said the Intelligence chief. "So Jim and I can get ourselves hidden
away in the storage compartments."

Penny nodded, smiled and closed herself in the
cab.

Sitting on a folding stool, McGuinness spread out
his quickly drawn maps of Stallion's Reach. "A
charming young girl," he said. "Isn't she?"

"Yes," agreed Haley.

"These donuts aren't bad either."

"See?" said the computer.

From a slot in the trailer door Haley, breath held,

watched Penny slow the truck and stop at the first checkpoint. They had arrived at the foot of a sharply ascending mountain road, their way blocked by a wooden fence and gate. The gate was tended by a small brittle man in a worn denim work suit. The fence bore a sign reading: OCEAN VIEW POTTERY WORKS & KILN. PRIVATE. Haley couldn't hear Penny as she leaned from the cab window and gave the first of the passwords. Behind him Chief McGuinness was murmuring into a communications mike.

The brittle man walked away from the truck, moving hesitantly, and went to the gate locks. He opened the gate, pushed it, grimacing, wide open. He waved the truck and trailer through, his hand not rising higher than his chest.

Haley sighed, got his pistol in his hand and said quietly, "We're through the first gate."

McGuinness brushed powdered sugar from the rough maps he had resting on his knees. "This next will be the tough one. There are six Mankill sentries in this gatehouse just beyond the iron gates. And only you and me to render them harmless."

The truck was slowing, climbing uphill, roaring hard. "This reminds me," remarked the computer, "of the time we went after John Dillinger at the Little Bohemia Lodge up in Wisconsin in the spring of 1934. Those were the great days for us G-Men."

"Once we have control of the next gate, we can bring in our ground forces," said McGuinness. He cocked his head at the computer. "Is there any more coffee?"

"All out of coffee," replied the machine. "How

about hot chocolate? I have real Dutch chocolate. You remember when there was a place called Holland? Well, that was where they made Dutch chocolate."

Haley returned to the slot. Penny sensed it and smiled quickly over her shoulder. The truck pulled louder and then began to strain less. The road was leveling out, running flat between red rocky hills. Suddenly Penny was braking. Angling his head differently, Haley caught sight of two girls in the road, out of uniform but armed with blaster rifles. Penny acknowledged them with a quirky salute and spoke to them.

Haley waited, then noticed one of the Mankill girls grin. The two of them moved out of the roadway and the truck rolled on. The road slanted down now and the hillsides looked drier and rockier. The scrub brush had a faded, burned out look. Five minutes further on there came a high, heavy black iron fence and gate to stop them.

The Lady Day girl behind the gate wore black tunic and trousers and had a gold handled pistol strapped to her upper thigh. She scooped at the air with one beckoning hand and ordered Penny out of the cab and over to the fence. Haley lost Penny from view the first half minute she was gone from the driver's seat. Then he saw her again, standing one hand on hip in the brightening morning road. The exchange of passwords and countersigns was slow, seemed stretched and extended. Haley felt sweat forming across his back. His breathing was no longer automatic.

Penny came back along the road finally, stuck her tongue into her left cheek for an instant. She climbed in and started the truck. More slow time went by before the gates opened. The truck and computer trailer jerked and went ahead.

As soon as they were clear through the gateway Penny swung the rig hard off the road and into the gate house. The cab and trailer snaked around the cottage size guard building and blocked its five windows and single door.

Haley ran to the rear of the trailer. Pistol in hand, he stepped out onto the Stallion's Reach plateau.

Following him out, Chief McGuinness said, "Let's hope we can capture this first batch of girls."

They did. But there was still Lady Day.

XXV

To REACH the tower at the edge of the sea Haley had to move through a grove of willow trees. Low tangled branches, sharp slender leaves. Haley and five Special Commandos made a half circle, sweeping slowly ahead toward the high gray stone tower. Haley was at the far left of the string of advancing men.

As he progressed toward Lady Day's tower he

heard, faintly under the sounds of skirmishing back at the Mankill barracks, metal clicking on stone. Haley stooped low, angled further away from the commandos, aimed himself at the four story high stone fort. Behind the last of the trees he stopped, watching.

The bottom rung of a rope and metal tube ladder ticked once more against gray stone, six feet above the sandy ground behind the tower. A tall slender Negro girl, pretty and a foggy gray color, was nearly down the ladder. She fell wide legged and catlike from the final rung to the ground. She wore flared tan trousers, a pale blue sailing jacket and a pale blue scarf made a band for her long straight hair. When she spun and ran across the sandy ground to the cliff edge Haley spotted a small black leather holster strapped to her waist. She let herself over the side of the five hundred foot high cliff. Brush and scrub rattled.

Haley, checking the tower, crossed to the edge. No one else came down from the tower and only silence was in it now. He spread himself out and took a look over. The Negro girl was halfway down, facing forward toward the bright ocean, using a narrow thorny path. About three hundred yards from the end of the path was a wooden boathouse with a long plank pier projecting out into the water. A small motor launch bobbed at the pier's end. This tiny slim stretch of beach was cut off at either end by palisades of sharp black rock and scatters of boulders.

The running girl was nearly to the beach when

Haley started after her. He moved downward faster than he'd intended, losing his footing and sliding down, scattering rocks and breaking off twists of brush and thorn vine.

The girl heard and turned. She unseamed her jacket and it flapped open. Then she drew her small pistol free and sent a blast at Haley. The shot missed, burning up scrub.

Haley closed up like a sourbug and rolled and tumbled downhill. He hit the sand two hundred feet to the left of the girl. He got off a shot as he came up to a standing position. He aimed at the Negro girl's legs, but missed her entirely.

She fired again, not catching him, and then ran for the boathouse. Haley ran, too, his dash paralleling hers. He was in among black rocks when she went shouldering into the white shingle building.

Haley got himself into a secure place to watch and shoot from. "Lady Day," he called out.

A window slammed up. "What?"

"You must have noticed the cops and soldiers up there. You're not going to make it clean away."

"You look like you must be Haley."

"That's right."

"What you ought to be worrying about is Penny. You ought to worry about what she did when she was one of us. About who she slept with."

Haley didn't reply.

Quiet grew.

High up in the clear sky gulls circled and harshly called. The surf hissed across the sand.

Wood creaked.

Haley shifted, listening hard. He sensed a shuffling on the beach beyond the boathouse. In a few moments, from among the rocks further to his left a blaster fired at him. The shot was two arm lengths wide of him. Lady Day had apparently left the boathouse through its underside and climbed up behind him.

Haley rolled again, putting a high, wide boulder between him and the gray girl. The beach didn't exist here. There was only rock and boulders, flush with the sea.

"Doesn't that interest you, Haley? You look too straight not to be upset. Penny is not what you imagine at all."

Haley stayed quiet, edging gradually upward, keeping hidden.

"Why don't you talk back, you poor son of a bitch of a cop?"

Carefully Haley, flat to the ground, made his way higher.

"Nobody can really love a dyke, can they? Isn't that what you feel, you poor son of a bitch of a cop?"

Haley gradually got several hundred feet away from where Lady Day thought he was.

"But I know what you think. All of you. From the time you killed my family eleven years ago, right in the street. I wasn't grown up then and I wasn't Lady Day and I got away. I've been aware, since then, of how it is. You can kill people, right in the street, right in the open, for simply trying to get what's due. All you have to say is you're the authority and they're the riot. Well, killing isn't just yours anymore. Sometime maybe, when all this is mine, Frisco Enclave and all, then maybe nobody will get killed for wanting food. Nobody will get shot down or gassed by men, men in uniform. That's what's coming. How does that sound, you poor son of a bitch of a cop?"

Haley came down behind Lady Day, clipped the pistol from her hand and said, "Okay, relax now."

The pretty gray girl's nostrils flared and she swung a hard uppercut at him. "You're always and always trying to prove you're a man!" she cried. "All of you, all of you killing people to prove it."

Haley moved and caused her to miss. He grabbed her wrist, said, "Enough. You're caught."

She writhed and twisted for a long moment, then grew still. "I figured to goad you into showing yourself. After you did I could kill you and take my boat out of here." She pointed. "That's a very nice boat, isn't it? First one I could ever afford. It's pretty. God bless the child who's got his own."

"You got too interested in talking about yourself," said Haley. "It can spoil things."

"Lots of people have been talking about me," said Lady Day. "They'll keep right on. I'm not over."

Haley said, "Let's go back over there now."

After he turned her over to the Special Commandos, Haley stayed on the beach. He walked close to the water, stopped and looked toward the ocean, toward the hazy horizon. A small yacht, brilliant white and trimmed in intense blue, was approaching from the north.

In awhile Penny came down the hillside and joined Haley. "You're okay?"

"I'm fine, yes."

"That was Lady Day?"

"Seems to be."

"What's her real name?"

"I didn't ask."

The blue and white yacht was now even with them, about a quarter mile out. At the rail a shaggy naked man was waving signal flags. Penny noticed and said, "Is that a new threat?"

Haley narrowed his eyes. "It looks more like La Penna."

"What's he signaling?"

"He says: 'Congratulations! I'm enroute to Tijuana to finish my job. Look at the boobs on this broad.'"

"What broad?"

"There she is by the lifeboat."

"Oh, yes."

Haley and Penny waved a greeting at La Penna and the yacht sailed by southward.

Penny said then, "You've already finished your job. Do we stay together?"

Haley smiled. "We do."

"Good. Though it's going to take some work," said the girl. "By the way, I like this new smile of yours better than the old grin."

"So do I," said Haley and smiled again.

MORE SCIENCE FICTION ADVENTURE!